MW01007072

THE COUNTING HOUSE

Also by David Dabydeen

Fiction:
The Intended
Disappearance
A Harlot's Progress
Our Lady of Demerara

Poetry:
Slave Song
Coolie Odyssey
Turner

Non-fiction:
Hogarth's Blacks: Images of Blacks in Eighteenth Century English Art
Hogarth, Walpole and Commercial Britain

DAVID DABYDEEN

THE COUNTING HOUSE

PEEPAL TREE

First published in Great Britain in 1996
by Jonathan Cape Ltd

This revised edition published in 2005
Peepal Tree Press Ltd
17 King's Avenue
Leeds LS6 1QS
England

Copyright © 2005, David Dabydeen

ISBN 1 84523 015 9

All rights reserved
No part of this publication may be
reproduced or transmitted in any form
without permission

ARTS COUNCIL
ENGLAND   Peepal Tree gratefully acknowledges Arts Council support

For Janet Jagan, her son Cheddi Jr ('Joey')
and Anna Rutherford

the King was in the counting house
counting out his money
the Queen was in the parlour
eating bread and honey
the maid was in the garden
hanging out the clothes
when down came a blackbird
and pecked off her nose

ACKNOWLEDGMENTS

I am grateful to Marjorie Davies for typing and retyping manu-
scripts; and to Michelle Rembrance, once again, for the fierceness
with which she helped shape this novel.

'When I enquired of them the nature of their grievances, a hundred Negro and Indian voices arose, vying against each other to tell a story, like crabs in a sack seeking escape by clambering over each other. I called upon them to speak in turn, assuring them that I would give each story equal weight and benign consideration, but my words fell on deaf ears. I mounted my horse and departed, leaving the loudest to bully the rest into silence.'

Mr Fielding

'No account of coolie experience can ever be complete for they are the scraps of history.'

Mr Gladstone

African slaves were freed in the West Indies in 1838, and between then and 1917 the British shipped half-a-million Indians ('coolies') to the region as replacement labour. Specially appointed native recruiters lured peasants to the West Indian plantations by promises of quick wealth and fertile land. The Indian Mutiny of 1857 also led to mass migration.

In the ruined counting house of Plantation Albion, British Guiana, three small parcels of materials survive as the only evidence of the nineteenth-century Indian presence. The first two parcels consist mostly of lists of Indian names, accounts of the wages paid to them, and scraps of letters. The contents of the third parcel are a cow-skin purse, a child's tooth, an ivory button, a drawing of the Hindu God, Rama, haloed by seven stars, a set of iron needles, some kumari seeds, and an empty tin marked 'Huntley's Dominion Biscuits', its cover depicting a scene of the Battle of Waterloo.

PART I

ROHINI

Rohini swept and re-swept the hut, rinsed and dried their two plates and cups, then searched around for more work. She reached for the cutlass and began to chop the firewood into even smaller pieces. She wanted to rest but her hands fretted, like Vidia fretting over his money, wanting more, wanting a sack stuffed with coins, or a belly stuffed with child. For the moment he saved his money in glass jars buried under a calabash tree. They were perfectly safe there. He took his chances with the spirits which lived in the branches, no longer bothering to leave a spoonful of sugar or a lily-leaf of fresh cow's milk at the base of the tree as an offering to ward off their malice. The living, thieving coolies were more dangerous than they. The jars were originally clear, but he painted them black as if to keep even the worms from gazing upon his money and turning it into stone. At the end of each week he went out into the darkness, dug them up, and brought them back to the hut. He would wait for hours for the clouds to discourage the moon, and no coolie was in sight, before returning the jars. She watched him come and go, pitying his habit. When he laid out the coins she felt a sudden compassion for the smallness of his fortune, the meagre piles of copper which rose a mere few inches from the surface of the table. At the same time she hated his ambitiousness, the foolishness of it. She remembered when they first saw the city of Calcutta, his eyes straining with greed for the bigness of the buildings, as if he wanted all of them to belong to him. They had walked for sixteen days from their village in Kandeera, dozens of them heading to the depot to be registered as emigrants to Guiana. Each village on the way looked like their own: a group of mudhuts set down in baked or waterlogged earth, each as paltry as his pile of coins. Goats wandered through the litter of excrement, rags, balls of straw, eating everything, even sniffing at the children put out to play in the dirt. Rohini was born

13

in such circumstances, and her mother and grandmother before her. Her inheritance was secure until the day the recruiter came and filled her head with fable.

'Guiana is the very land of Ramayana. Ramayana set in long-time-ago place, and the whitepeople them now plough it, and they call it Guiana. And it have so much gold there that you don't have enough hand and neck and foot to wear bangle. You wish you had ten hands like Lord Shiva, and even then you run out of skin.'

'That is one stupidness you talking. If Guiana so rich, why you not go there yourself?' the village-elder asked.

'You never hear of Mukti?' the recruiter retorted, playing on their ignorance. 'Only backward people don't know that Lord Rama call on some of us to serve and sacrifice. We call Mukti because we give up good fortune in this life to live worse than chamar. It is nothing but blessing we want, to bathe in the shadow of Lord Rama.' And he turned his eyes upwards, touched his forehead and made other elaborate gestures of obeisance.

This is how Rohini remembered him, doing his duty to God. She wanted so much to believe but the elder took up a stick and chased him. 'Gwan, gwan, gwan swine-keeper, else I break your neck!' And the recruiter picked up his sack in a weary motion, like one doomed to the rejection of infidels. Before leaving, though, he went up to the elder with meek demeanour, bowed extravagantly, and touched his feet. But this final appeal was wasted, the elder stretching out his hand to dismiss him.

A few days later, when the elder was away on a goodwill visit to the next village, the recruiter appeared mysteriously. 'All of you come, come, all of you,' he called, beckoning people to him. He blew a cow-horn slung from his waist to alert the men working in the fields. 'In this sack here,' he said, 'is magic. Ramayana. Guiana. White magic. You ever hear thunderclap? Well, whitepeople capture the thunder in the whole sky and put it in one piece of iron. Look!' And he reached into his sack and withdrew a pistol. It was the first time any of them had seen one. He held it up high above his head for people to marvel at, but it looked so meek that some women began to giggle. 'Girl!' He pointed at Rohini. She hid behind her mother but he kept his eyes

14

on her. 'You there! Is it you I hear laugh? God let go one curse on you for laughing. You want God blight your belly so you don't born child?'

'Shut your mouth, you mad-rass man,' her mother screamed, hugging the child protectively to her. And suddenly the man pointed the thing to the peepul tree in the middle of the village and fired. Birds scattered. People scattered. Rohini fell and somebody stepped on her mouth and broke off a tooth. She started to bleed. A hen scrambled in the mud beside her. All she could see was a spout where its head was shot clean off. It hopped sideways and shuddered and flapped and kicked and the whole place was quiet; everyone was hiding in hut or in ditch staring at the hen pouring out bile. She lay there calling out to her mother but no word came, and the man was walking towards her with his sack opened, as if he wanted to kidnap her, and when he reached her, he took out two ripe mangoes and pieces of panap and gave them to her to eat. 'Take. Take. No frighten. It is only gun.' And he forced the fruit and sweets in her lap whilst she shuddered and flapped and kicked and the whole place was still quiet. She was bleeding as he stood over her. She could see his eye looking at her nipple. 'Who this child belong to?' he asked in a soft voice, looking around the empty village as if he wanted to offer money for her. She hated this man. Nasty money-minded bitch! Her Pa was dead, otherwise he would come out and bap! and cuff recruiter in the face and break off both hands that now reached out to pick her up and pat her. Her tooth was broken but she would bite him yet if he touched her bubby. She hated this man. She hated all of them, except Vidia who, even when she didn't ask, hurried to pick water-coconut when she thirsted and ripe running papaya to quench her mouth.

When Rohini turned seventeen, her mother, Finee, married her to Vidia. The pandit intoned the usual story of Seta's banishment and her eventual reconciliation with Lord Rama, skipping over details so as to finish early and get to the food. Iron pots bubbling with potato curry and dhall, wooden trays bearing water-melons, mangoes and jilips... most of Finee's life-savings squandered in a day. She would die, though, knowing that she had fulfilled her duty in successfully marrying off her only girl-child, as her own mother had once done for her. But Jagnat, her husband, had been a different boy from this Vidia. He was scarred everywhere, thick lines dividing his skin in patchwork fashion. The villagers said that God had started on him in too much of a hurry to bother with perfection. God had joined this piece, that piece, anything left over from other people's making. The needle sewed crudely so all the borders showed. But for all Jagnat's ugliness she had done well by him. True, God hadn't put sufficient cord in his back so it was permanently slack. As to his nose, the bone was too small to support all that flesh, so it drooped like the comb of a hen. She cried when her mother first suggested she should marry him, but the dowry was reduced according to his physical damage, so it was a good match for her family. Instead of a cow, four ducks and several brass pots, his family was offered a few hens too old to lay and some rupees to salvage their pride.

Jagnat had been a grateful husband, working without complaint in the fields, never beating her, and making shy, ineffectual advances in bed. He fumbled in the dark, and from a respectable distance. He would not allow their upper bodies to meet and they never kissed in case she sucked the flesh of his nose by accident. Nor could she fondle him under his vest lest her hands discovered the misshapen contours of his body. After the birth of Rohini he gave up sleeping with her altogether, his duty fulfilled. He died

16

less than a year afterwards, inevitably, from the effort of living. He barely survived to see the miracle he had spawned, a child without blemish. In life he had provided faithfully for her, giving her an unmarked child. In death he had left her without the shame of widowhood, his obvious deformities ensuring that no one blamed her for the brief sickness that killed him.

Finee watched the two of them playing, Vidia rolling a gurmit seed along the ground, trying to guide it into a hole Rohini had dug. The seed hovered on the rim, refusing to drop, and Rohini squawked at his failure, grabbing the seed as her prize. Vidia never complained, always letting her have her way. 'My tongue dry, go pick me papaya,' she demanded, and off he ran to fetch the fruit. Every afternoon he returned from the field, where he looked after his father's goats, with a pocketful of gurmits. Rohini received his gifts nonchalantly as if they were a tribute due to her. The greater her calmness the greater his desire to serve her, and as Finee watched the two of them she knew she would soon be impoverished. She would have to sell the only piece of jewellery she still possessed – a silver anklet slipped off her mother's dead foot – and the cow Jagnat left for her, to provide Rohini's dowry. If only Vidia was disfigured! But no, the boy was fair-skinned and smooth-faced, with thick, healthy, black hair which shone with coconut oil. Each morning his mother, Droopatie, sat him prominently at the front of their hut and rubbed oil into his hair. She was displaying him to the village, advertising his worth. A bull, two cows and new gold for her nose and wrists. Of course, in a season of flood or drought she would part with him for less, but whilst the sun shone upon green, irrigated fields, and the men reaped without the least sign of dysentery to weaken them, and the women wove mats to be sold in the bazaars of Calcutta, and the children were without lice, then she would obtain the full asking price. No one would dare bargain with her.

What Droopatie didn't reckon on, however, was her son's weakness for Rohini. As soon as he was loosened from her grip he found himself drawn to Rohini's hut, letting the goats run ahead whilst he paused to present her with a bright-blue button ripped secretly from his mother's blouse, or a piece of wood which he had spent all night carving into a god. 'Marry Mala. Her family own five heifers and a bull to tear their arse with breeding!' Droopatie pleaded, but Vidia turned his face from her. 'What wrong with Mala, you stupid boy?' she asked, pulling his hair and on the verge of slapping sense into him. But he remained stubborn in his devotion to Rohini. The more Droopatie bawled at him the more determinedly he stole from her to give to Rohini, so that at the beginning of the marriage season Rohini had already amassed a handkerchief of white linen, the god Hanuman fashioned from a slice of sandalwood, a peacock feather plucked from a bouquet which his mother had fastened on the wall to lighten the gloom of the hut, and four buttons – one carved in ivory which he had discovered at the bottom of the trunk in which she kept the family's heirlooms. Vidia made his own box for Rohini to house her treasures, a miniature version of his mother's trunk. He squatted in the field ignoring the goats, concentrating instead on binding twigs with bird-lime and twine, shaping them into a box which he lined with cotton ripped secretly from Droopatie's best sari. She wore it ostentatiously to funerals. The only villager threatening to die, though, was Kumar, but he was more old than sick. He would last, being mean and miserable and living alone, grinding his gums and shooing away any animal that wandered into his yard, cursing children that walked by for being young, prophesying that this one would be barren, that one would develop leprosy – so Vidia calculated that it would be some time yet before Kumar died and the ruined sari was discovered.

Finee watched them playing, the gurmit seed running smoothly from Vidia's hand towards the hole and Rohini waiting with open mouth as it hovered on the rim. If only Finee could break his arm in three places to make his aim crooked. If only when he stooped to roll the marble she could put a spell on him to keep him in that posture for ever. But he was delicate in all his movements, from the way he caressed the seed in his palm to the way he released it along the ground. He raised his body gently and walked after it, remaining composed even though Rohini was a flurry of energy, like fowl about to be fed. Her hand pecked at the seed and she ran off greedily.

'Rohini! Rohini! Come here! Stop that stupidness and come right now!' She would interrupt their play for the sake of it. All her life she milked, fetched water, swept, darned, cooked, cleaned pot, and for what? For some smooth-faced boy to come and demand dowry for her daughter and leave the mother lonely and bangle-less, not one nose-ring nor piece of silver left? What did this life give her but a husband? 'Go clean out the fireside!' she ordered, and Rohini went sullenly to the kitchen. Vidia lingered outside the hut, unsure of whether to wait for Rohini or go home. Finee reached for a piece of cloth and began to sew, trying her best to ignore him. She saw him pick up a stick and gouge holes idly in the earth. She dug her needle into the cloth as if piercing Jagnat's sores. It was like this in the last weeks of his life – blossoms of pus upon his skin and she having to prick them. She hated his sickness then, wishing a quick death upon him. Day after day she tended him, her needle poised at his skin as if it were poor cloth needing to be mended. What God undid she had to stitch together. What had she done God that He should mock her with a man unravelling every moment unto death, whilst she had to struggle to sew him together with a simple iron needle? Imagine, a simple iron needle! Why didn't God fight her fairly, give her a hundred rupees so that at least she could bring the best doctor from Calcutta with a bag full of medicines? If Jagnat still died even though his stomach was crammed with pills and syrups, then God could smile in triumph. But what victory was there in beating an empty-handed woman?

'Boy, don't idle at my door, get out of my sight!' she squawked at Vidia, wishing the needle was a cutlass with which to chase him all the way home. Vidia dropped his stick. He cast a last shameful look into the hut in the hope of sighting Rohini, but Finee blotted the doorway.

She watched him walk slackly down the path to his own home. Now that she had punctured his pride she began to pity him. At least he was an obedient boy, never raising a complaint however much she abused him. She could do worse than marry Rohini to him. Next time he came round she would search out in the trunk what was left in Jagnat's tobacco pouch and give him some to chew. She might even touch his fresh skin as she did Jagnat's sack

19

towards the end. Semi-conscious and prostrate for days he had suddenly flexed upright, his mouth meeting hers. She cradled his head in her arms, overcome with gratitude for the marriage she had so often despised. Then, when he died, she held his head for a long while before letting it slip from her, so that she could once again feel the weight of being empty-handed.

Finee swept the mud ground of her hut in rage. She would sweep dust all along the village road, building up a heap of rubble to deposit at Droopatie's door, if she had her way. Bird-shit more odorous than the nastiness in that woman's heart! And look how like whore she behave! She sit in her yard combing and oiling that boy's hair, leaning over him so all her breasts loosen from her blouse for all the world to see. Not one button to keep them in place. Any decent wife would sew on a few in self-respect, but no, no button, not for that big-bosom bitch! All-man passing and peeping, and her husband planting all day don't know one thing. Is licks she looking for. If her husband Harilall only know, is cuff and cutlass chop and then you will see mayhem in this place. How dare she scorn *my* situation, calling *my* husband a cripple who dead out as soon as girl-child born? A louse like that! She breed one son, then her womb close up and no more boy-pickni come, no matter how hard her husband huff. All night he pumping but she stubborn, sterile; he might as well try planting rice in sand. And now he run out of water, he start to wither up, and become scrawny like locust and cockroach-leg and all those people we hear starving in Bihar. Meanwhile her bubby swell full and snap the button and flop out of her blouse, inviting other man. And she want dowry for Vidia to marry my daughter? A shameless cross-eye scunt like that! Well, even if I own a herd so plenty that numbers not sufficient to count them, she is not getting one meagre calf, not even calf-foot, much less calf-tail. Calf-shit, yes, but even then she have to haggle hard.

'Why your mother only scowl at me?' Vidia asked timidly, dreading her answer, but Rohini merely stared at the movement of his lips. 'Whenever she see me she start fretting and pick up her broom. I hurry past her, just in case.'

'Just in case I kiss you, what you will do?' Rohini asked softly.

'What?'

'You know what to do? You know how to move your mouth and everything?' Her eyes fastened again on his lips.

His father's goats raised their faces to the sun as if to chew. Two months without rain had reduced the field to patches of grass which the goats had almost completely devoured. He looked out at his inheritance, wondering whether it was enough for her. Would they die out in a drought and leave him without gifts? Girls usually raised the dowry but he wanted nothing from her. He would give everything instead.

'Come to the tamarind tree,' she said, rising and reaching for his hand.

'Why?'

'Because it lonely there…'

He hesitated, looking dutifully at the goats but she tugged at him. He got up and followed her. She skipped over the dry trench and took the short-cut path from the field. The clay was pebbly and hot and stung his feet but she hurried ahead. 'Here,' she said, guiding him to the spot, her eyes alert even in the sudden shadowiness of the tree's cover, 'here will do.' He sat down automatically and she knelt before him and moved her face towards his. 'Quick, before anybody come.'

'Who will come?' he asked, shifting as if to get up but she wouldn't let him move. She put her mouth upon his. It opened unexpectedly and his tongue made to escape but she chased after it and caught it between her lips. He tried to retrieve it but she clamped more firmly.

'You hurting me!' he gurgled, but she took his indistinct words as an expression of pleasure until he pushed her violently and she fell. She lay on the ground wanting to cry. She was glad for the darkness; he would not see her crying.

Vidia was relieved that it was all over. 'I sorry,' he said, addressing the branches overhead.

'Sorry for what?' she asked casually, as if nothing had happened or nothing he did could distress her.

'Because I don't know how,' he said, continuing to speak to the tree.

'Me as well,' she admitted readily, humoured by his honesty.

22

'You mean to say what you just do is not how?'

'No… only sometimes.'

'But how then?'

'My Pa long dead, I never big enough to see how he do it with Ma. You never see your Ma and Pa?'

'Then how you find out about kiss and thing?' he asked, brushing aside her question.

'I just do. How baby snake know to poison though it just born?'

'How come goat and them don't kiss, or sheep and cow?' he persisted, eager to test her knowledge. 'When last you see fowl and duck and them doing it? Not even my Ma and Pa does kiss.'

'What? Even your Ma and Pa?' She laughed, knowing that he was lying. 'What they do instead?'

'They act like goat. How else you expect it? He jump on her and tumble her up till noise come, then he climb off, lie down and puff.'

'And then what happen?'

'Nothing. He sleep. She sleep sometimes but mostly she get up and go to the kitchen to grind massala or make dough for tomorrow roti.'

Rohini leaned towards him and stuck out her tongue. 'Put your tongue on my tongue,' she instructed. He turned away instead, screwed up his eyes and concentrated on the goats in the field, counting and re-counting them in his mind. Four, but two might get pregnant, which will make six. One for each of his sisters and the ram-goats for himself, if his parents died today. Plus a share in the cows, and ducks and whatever jewellery was hidden in the trunk. She deserved more. I is nothing, worse than grass, I might as well have four foot and bleat, he wanted to confess to her.

'Come close,' she said, but half-heartedly, put off by the stupid expression on his face. Are all of them stupid? Like her father? Would she become like her mother, hard-hearted, uncertain in mood, angry one moment then expansively forgiving the next?

'Man is God's curse. Good-for-nothing and burdensome,' Finee fretted, stabbing her needle into the cloth. 'As to your Pa…' She leaned back to think deeply on her husband, the lines around her mouth drawn together in a knot of bitterness. 'If I could have live in a different world and have choice, then it is cockroach I prefer to be than wife. Cockroach, rat, mongoose, weevil, anything but wife.' On other occasions Finee would squat at the corner of the hut and suddenly cry for Jagnat, remembering aloud the tenderness with which she had massaged his legs, wishing away the rottenness of muscle that made him limp. 'Your Pa had heart strong like bull though the rest of him fray and running. That man love me so much that he harness all his energy for two years' marriage, and then his breath blow short, and he loose his yoke and gone.' She rocked her body and moaned. She curled her arms to hold his imagined head, lowering her face to kiss his eye. Rohini watched her as she enacted the dying, the shuddering, the sporadic vomiting, the way Jagnat's mouth finally jolted upright to meet hers in a grotesque and involuntary romance.

'Kiss me now,' Rohini demanded, and without waiting for a response ran her tongue along the side of Vidia's face. He let her do it. He had seen the cow doing it to her young. He put out his and licked her in turn.

'What is wrong?' he asked as she pulled away.

'Nothing,' she said, nauseated by the feel of his wet tongue.

'What is wrong?' he insisted against his will. He preferred not to know. He felt small and shameful again. He looked away from her into the darkness of the tree's cover. She sensed his hurt and touched him again in spite of her mother's warning.

'Holding your Pa was like if you embrace a leper,' Finee cursed when the mood took her and she giggled uncontrollably. 'I couldn't hug him too tight lest he start leak. I couldn't pull him to me lest something snap off and I left forever clutching some finger or ear or eyeball. Rohini, watch out for man. Even when they look firm with promise, deep down all of them septic.'

Still Rohini drew Vidia to her, pressed his head so tightly to her neck that she could feel a trickle of oil.

'Kiss my shoulder,' she ordered and he obeyed. 'Where else you want to lick?' she asked.

'I don't know. Where else people lick?'

'I don't know.'

'Me neither.'

And they both fell into a grievous silence.

'You want do with me what you see ram-goat do?' she asked after a while, the contempt welling up again inside her.

When Finee saw Vidia by the village pond she knew immediately that there was danger in his body, that he would irritate her with the memory of her husband's imperfection. His gentle, almost groomed movements only made her suspect him of unruliness, temptation, vulgar demands. He lay on the bank until the sun dried him, then he went back into the pond. Dressing or undressing, it was the restraint of Vidia's gestures which affected her, the temporary withholding of passion. He would grow up to become a torment to whoever married him, his assurance provoking in his wife a desire to hurt him; at the same time, guilt for having such malign thoughts, and fear that another woman would win him by submitting her body unconditionally. At least with Jagnat there had been no such complications. He merely sought his meals and clean clothes and someone to wipe the dribble from the sides of his mouth when his time came to die. There was no lust in him waiting to be expressed. He measured his wants according to the capacity of his body, and realising that he was ugly he settled for simple caring. His containment was unlike Vidia's for there was little to violate. When Jagnat eventually breached Finee they made a baby and that was the end of his sexual feeling for her. He had fulfilled his duty. The surprise was that she managed to stay with him and after a while even wanted to. Was it because he let her spend the nights on her own, making no demands of her? Did she want to be alone? She would lie awake and listen to him breathing. He did so, as with all his other motions in life, uncouthly. Everything was difficult for him, and she pitied one so abused, so undeservedly punished. The pity of it satisfied her. It made her feel purposeful and she protected him against humiliation by not complaining, by not revealing her own wants. But what *did* she want? She didn't know. She could have known if she dwelt on the question, but she wouldn't, concentrating instead on his breathing as if it were coming from her own body. She sought out his pain, to make it hers, to make it the only source of satisfaction in her life. Sometimes his breathing was uneven – there would be a long pause between one gasp and another. She panicked then at the thought of his death. What would be left to her once he took his pain elsewhere, reborn in some other woman's lap as a vomiting infant? But perhaps he would not come back sickly. In the next life he could be the pleasurable image of a landlord. Ha! However he turned out, though, he would have betrayed her by belonging to another woman. For the first time in her relationship with him she felt jealous.

'Don't let Vidia do anything,' Finee warned Rohini, 'like touch you naked. Button your clothes all the time.'

'But Ma, I getting married to him next month.'

Finee scowled at her. 'You want your belly swell up?'

'Swell up how?'

'Swell up, just wait and see. All they want is boy-child, like themselves. Ten children they want and still not content. Don't give them nothing, you hear, nothing. Here, take this.' She rifled through a sack under the bed until she found a small, cotton parcel. She untied it to reveal a set of dried kumari seeds. 'Swallow one with fresh milk after he do it with you to block up your passage. Best to be barren. He'll want you always then and not betray you. Once you have baby you will grow fat like me – you want to grow ugly like your Ma? You want your bubby to get slack? What you know about man and woman business?'

'Nothing, Ma,' she lied, for she had already undressed before Vidia. All afternoon under the cover of the tamarind tree she made him do things with her until she grew bored with his addiction and the little noises escaping from his mouth. She withdrew her breasts and sent him back to his goats.

'Man and woman business messy. And Vidia cunning, he will get inside your stomach and make sickness. The boy is strong and get control and you will be the one to bawl. He will take over you and put you to work in the nights to please him. You will be like a plateful of food for him.'

Rohini looked at her mother, wanting to laugh. Vidia strong? How could her mother be so stupid as to believe that Vidia was strong enough to enslave her?

'When man lie on top of you, it is like if you bury alive. You can't breathe, you can't scream, dirt fill up your mouth.'

But Rohini knew otherwise, lying on her back, taking Vidia's hand and putting it between her thighs. The more he closed his fingers around her, the more the pleasure leaked from her. He could never staunch the flow nor contain it in his closed palm.

'Better you marry someone with four cow, four sheep and four tired limbs, too old to lock round you at night.'

'Why you don't marry me off to Kumar?' Rohini jeered. 'He get no teeth and claw and he ready to drop dead. Just because Pa cripple don't mean I must marry like you.'

'Sssch your mouth!' her mother scolded her. 'Don't speak so brazen about your father! That man was a saint considering what God make him bear.'

'You only want Vidia for yourself,' Rohini blurted out, stopping her mother's drift into sentimental memory. Finee looked at Rohini in disbelief. The child was declaring herself a rival woman; the child who at birth gave her status in the eyes of the village, proving her to be fertile, lessening the shame of her marriage to an unwanted creature. For sixteen years after Jagnat's death, Rohini had been her companion in drudgery, fetching water, grating coconut, scrubbing pot and karahi, selling milk, beating other people's clothes. These were years of barest subsistence, except at festival time when Finee gathered together leftover scraps of cloth and sewed them into a costume so that Rohini could play Radha. She sewed furiously to invent an outfit which would dazzle everyone, but especially outdo Vidia's Krishna costume. Each year he played Lord Krishna, his mother sparing no expense to dye his body and decorate him in flowers. It vexed her that Finee's daughter played Radha, but it was the decision of the village council to cast Radha as the sibling of poverty, whose rise to divine favour would inspire all the other girls. Rohini automatically qualified for the part, living as she did in a ramshackle hut, its roof shedding more of its coconut branches as each year passed, and without a father to provide morality or dowry. That such a low-caste, dark-skinned, barefooted girl could be chosen by the gods to be one of the brides of creation showed that the gods cared for the wretchedness of humanity. All who suffered but remained virtuous would be rewarded in the next life. Finee watched Rohini clothed in coloured ribbons and sequined finery being paraded through the village on a painted cart, knowing that everything was make-believe but still wanting to believe. When the playing was over and they returned home, she gave the girl allowance to rest for the remainder of the week, doing all the scavenging in the garden, the peeling, the chopping of wood, the cooking and washing, the daubing of fresh mud to cover holes in the hut, the feeding of the animals, the mending of rags. She would not end the dream too quickly by setting the girl to all such labour that marked the beginning and end of days. Instead she let Rohini take out of the trunk all their treasure, their insurance against starvation, to polish: the silver anklet belonging to her mother, two brass lotas, an enamel plate painted with maharajas on elephants. She made Rohini shine them, all the time picturing the girl in a courtyard strewn with peacocks. But there was never in her mind an image of a youthful Lord Krishna to go with Radha. She was practical enough to know that Rohini would attract no such master, not in this lifetime. What rich family would marry their son to one so destitute, however gorgeous she appeared at the festival? Money, all they wanted was money, and she had none. Better for Rohini's consort to be a widower, someone with a few years to live who needed the scent of a fresh young woman; someone who, as he lay breathing on his death-bed, would watch all her quick movements as she busied herself in his home; the quickness of her hands and her clean nipples glimpsed as she bent over to feed him. In the year or two it took him to die Rohini would only be his servant, not his mistress, in spite of the gossip of the village. Once or twice Rohini could, if she felt compassionate, let the old man take her breasts in his mouth to comfort him in his misery. She could even massage between his legs when his pain became unbearable, but nothing else. She would preserve her virtue for the next life, when a real Lord Krishna might greet her, instead of a boy-player covered in tinsel. When the widower died he would leave Rohini sufficient money never to be dependent on another man. Finee would then build a larger house in several acres of land, and acquire a herd of cows. They would employ servants to plant a garden and a manager to sell the produce, or to lend the money to the villagers, making sure each rupee was repaid strictly with interest. No one was to be let off – not for all the curses they had breathed on Finee behind her back, especially Vidia's mother: that she was the wife of a hunchback with one hungry-bellied girl-child; that she wore cast-off clothing and broken sandals to her own husband's funeral; that she still owed the pandit five rupees for the prayers, so Jagnat's soul was frozen in space, unable to be reborn and marry a better woman than Finee; that the ghee she rubbed on Jagnat's corpse offended God for it was impure, mixed with mustard oil to save money.

So Finee dreamed of transformations which would make her matriarch of the village, chief money-lender and market gardener, with a beautiful daughter whom she would preserve from marriage. Let the suitors threaten to drink poison. Let them unwrap their dhotis, fasten them around their necks and make to hang themselves. Let them stand outside her gate, wailing or waving their rupees. They would wait there for ever before she conceded.

But now Rohini was glowering at her, demanding Vidia. Her daughter whom she wanted to remain a child now hinted at sexual rivalry. 'I only vow in my heart to keep you from man and shame. You want to get bilious and bear children? You want pain more than your first period?' she pleaded. 'Come, beti, come,' she beckoned Rohini, summoning up all her powers of cunning. She forced her eyes to water and her voice to falter. She made to sob, and to hold it back. She would feign an epileptic fit as the last resort. Rohini didn't budge though, unaffected by her mother's antics. She turned her face away and stared in the direction of Vidia's hut. It was then that Finee realised that all was lost, for the dowry would have to be found. A noise broke from her, willed at first but it soon took control of her, unpicking her eyes. She cried as she had done at Jagnat's funeral, shifting and modulating the tone of her grief, swelling its volume to an unbearable level until everyone present was convinced of the depth of her love for him and sought to comfort her. Even so, she had continued to wail for a good few minutes afterwards, awed by her own capacity for making noise, forcing her voice to an even higher pitch. Then, exhausted by the performance, she had brought it to an end by seeming to faint for the duration of the ceremony. They rushed to construct a palanquin and four men carried her all the way to the river bank, saving her the hour's hot walk. She awoke partially to light the cremation pyre, then she collapsed again and left them to supervise the stench, allowing herself to be lifted home in comfort.

'I want more,' Rohini told herself as she rolled roti under Droopatie's watchful eye. Now that the wedding was over and the bitterness on both sides subsiding, Droopatie was glad for Rohini's company. Her own four daughters had been married off. When the final tally was made, she had lost eight ducks and five cows in all the dowry transactions but had gained an obedient daughter-in-law. Rohini cooked sweetly, which was a blessing since Droopatie's hand was growing stiff with age. It was a bonus, after all, that she was dark-skinned and penniless for she would serve them faithfully for the rest of their lives.

'Bring me jilabie,' Droopatie ordered, and Rohini stopped whatever she was doing and went to the kitchen. Droopatie ate it ostentatiously, sighing at the deliciousness of the food and dipping her hand in the bowl of water Rohini had fetched. 'Beti, you make jilabie sweetest in this whole village. Lord Rama himself anoint your hand for cookery. What you think if we make jilabie and sell? I can then get money to buy new sari. I lose all respect when people dead and I have to wear rags to the funeral, because of that boy you marry. You hear how he did tear my clothes?'

Rohini nodded.

'From tomorrow I want you to take a tray of jilabie round the village and come back with at least five anna. Sari cost nine rupees, so year-end will come before I can show myself.'

'I want more,' Rohini brooded as she spat into the oil. She kneaded raisins into the flour and worked up a dough, spitting copiously into it. 'Lazy bitch! She treat me like slave but I disease her first!' From the kitchen window she could see her mother planting her garden. Finee looked underfed. Now that the cow had been surrendered to Droopatie there was no fresh milk to stave off malnutrition. The silver anklet had also gone so there was nothing with which to purchase special foods when illness

31

came. Finee would have to make do with whatever vegetables sprouted in the garden and in dry seasons, the remnants from neighbours' pots.

'I bring cooking oil and flour and sugar,' Rohini said, depositing her bag. 'Droopatie snoring but she soon will wake up so I can't stay long.'

'Seventeen years I bear you, you can stay how long you like.' Finee put away the haul, knowing that she only had a few minutes with her daughter. 'They treating you good?'

'Yes, Ma.'

'They working you hard?'

'No, Ma.'

'If she find out you steal from the kitchen and slap you, what you will do?'

'Nothing, Ma.'

'Nothing?'

'No, Ma.'

'Well, take some slaps and next time bring me some castor oil. I have worms.'

'Yes, Ma. Tomorrow.'

'God cruel. He provide me nothing yet He put worms in my belly to eat me up. Everything I eat, I eat for worms. I used to eat for you, you know that?'

'No, Ma.'

'When I was bloat up with you, Jagnat would climb tree for dounze and cherry. Eat, he say, eat for the child to grow strong. How that cripple did manage to climb tree is a miracle to this day! But he feed me, months and months, to make you big, and sometimes when food short he go without. He swallow spit to fill his stomach. You know that?'

'No, Ma.'

'Well, truth I talk. Go now in case that fire-rass jumbie wake up and scream at you. Go quick.'

'I want more than salt and flour and cooking oil,' Rohini vowed to herself as she undressed for Vidia. But what, she didn't know. She lay naked beside him, flinching each time he scooped her body.

'What wrong I do to you?' he whispered uncertainly. For a

32

whole week she had rejected him. He lay beside her feeling helpless and lonely. He wanted to rise from the floor, light a lamp and stay awake to talk to her, but his parents were in the bed a few feet away. Since the marriage there had been no space to talk to each other. From the time they awoke they led separate lives. She washed, and then went to the kitchen where she spent most of the day. After a brief, silent meal with his mother and father (Rohini only ate after they had finished) he took the family's cows and goats to the grazing field. He returned late into the afternoon, bathed, ate without her, then it was time to sleep. There were few chances to talk to her since there was no reason to enter the kitchen. When he did go there, to bring wood to the fireside or to repair the broken handle of a bucket, Droopatie always managed to find some excuse to be present. She would examine the grinding stone for grime or fuss over the crack opening up in the tawa. Vidia and Rohini moved about the kitchen awkwardly, trying not to catch each other's eye, not to touch each other accidentally. It was only at nights that he had her to himself, the two of them lying on the ground waiting endlessly for his parents to fall asleep, in the mean time not making the least movement under the rice sack covering.

'You sleeping?' he asked in the quietest of voices.

'No, you sleeping?'

'I don't want sleep. You?'

'Me too don't want sleep,' she replied, waiting for him to do something. But he was paralysed, as usual, by the nearness of his parents, so she forced him, running her fingers along his neck and chest. She moved his hand to her thighs and made him comb through them. She would torture him and be satisfied. She would arouse him, then gather the rice sack protectively around her body and turn away from him.

He retracted from his excitement and misery by dwelling, as usual, on the goats, recalling their names, their individual natures. There was Devi, always being mounted by Shiva but never giving birth like other people's goats. If only they could multiply and the herd grow to fourteen or twenty-eight. Then he could purchase his own plot and build his own hut and have his own wife to himself. Then there was Indra with ragged pelt and a permanent limp, whom Vidia named after the village beggar. Indrani was blind in one eye from an accident soon after birth. She had poked her head greedily into a discarded clay pot only to be bitten by a snake. Indrani never moved out of Indra's shadow, nibbling at whatever stump of grass he chose to leave behind. Theirs was a barren relationship, Indrani more interested in following him to sources of food than in mating.

What was he to do? Vidia agonised as Rohini turned her back to him. There seemed no escape from his parents who, in turn, were bound to the village and to the gods. They had pledged to maintain the temple, paying for the visiting pandit to conduct prayers. Such devotion gave them status in the eyes of the villagers who, out of respect, performed acts of service. When a strong wind appeared from nowhere to flatten half the village it was his parents' hut which was repaired first, though the damage was slight compared to the devastation suffered by others. When Indrani and Indra chewed their way out of the pen, wandered off into the night and disappeared into the bush, a party of villagers set off willingly the next day to retrieve them.

Vidia dwelt on the spectacle of Indrani and Indra being dragged home by ropes, on the sourness of their smell, the fleas which colonised their coats – any rank image to deaden his desire for Rohini. He could be content with her alone, break free of all the bonds imposed by his parents, the village, the gods, just to be loyal to her body. In three whole months of marriage he had only managed to mount her twice. Each time it was swift and frightening. The feeling rose and peaked and drained from him and he was left confused by the process. He wanted to cry out both times but his parents would awaken to scold him. As his hands roved over her body he plotted their escape, thinking up schemes for making money. Four recalcitrant goats would bring in nothing. Theft. But from whom would he steal? The only person in the village suspected of having money was Kumar but he had died penniless in spite of his promises to Vidia.

'You want make plenty pickni with Rohini?' he asked the boy, stopping him on his way to the fields.

'What business you got with we?' Vidia replied, suspicious of Kumar's sudden interest and kindly tone of voice. He had grown up fearing Kumar, a bearded old man in a torn dhoti who lived by himself at the edge of the village and spent most of the time sitting out in the sun, scratching his infested skin. He cursed whoever passed his gate, especially the young, by naming their blemishes. 'Girl, you, yes, you,' he called out, 'you with bow-leg as if egg hatching in your panty.' And the girl would be immobilised by his vulgarity. Before her malformed limbs could revive to carry her from his sight, Kumar would deliver the final blow, as if she were a cockroach he had only initially stunned. 'When period pain catch you,' he cackled at her, 'and your Ma stuff you with cloth, then we will really see how crooked you does walk.' Others suffered because of skinniness, sores or bulging eyeballs. He relished those with compounded ailments. It was as if he needed to feed off the energy of description to sustain his old age. 'Hear this riddle,' he hissed at one terrified child, 'solve it and you get one mouthful of sweetie from me. What bubble with boils more than pitch-lake, and blacker, and when sun hot it let off stink-vapour? You thinking hard? Don't think so hard because it is you, you tar-baby! You know you will die by the age of nine from breathing in your own foul breath?'

Vidia was one of the few who escaped ruination by Kumar. Whenever he passed Kumar's gate the old man would stop muttering and stare at the boy, even warning him to mind his ways. 'Watch where you walk today,' he shouted after him. 'Grass rife with snake. Quarter-moon last night and mist first thing this morning mean boa born, and mapapire, and coral.' And true enough, one bit into Indrani, sucking out the juice of her eye and injecting poison in its place. Vidia remained appalled by the appearance of Kumar – the crust of dirt on his skin and his permanently soiled clothing. After the snake bite, however, he paused to listen to whatever Kumar chose to utter. Kumar, seeing the boy approach, would grind his gums as if to work up froth for prophecy. 'Today, search well, you will find gift for Rohini under stone.'

'Which stone? Where it stay?'

'Find it yourself,' Kumar answered grumpily, as if he had changed his mind and the instinct to condemn the boy to a future of wretchedness had returned. He stared at a point in the air as if formulating something particularly savage. Vidia hurried away. All day he dug but the land was a sackful of stones that someone had emptied out carelessly. The sack held worms too and beetles and earth-lice. The stones rolled in different places and the insects scurried after them to hide from the sun. But the sun caught some of them before they could shelter, burning and hardening them into beads. How often in idleness had he cracked open a smaller stone with a larger stone and, instead of finding treasure, saw a trace of shell or what looked like the drawing of an insect? They fell from the sack, a ball of hairs and spidery limbs, hustling to find shade. His parents built a hut for cover, centipedes curled in obscure corners, worms sheltered under the stones of other worms. Everything was hiding from the face of the sun. But why should he remain as helpless as the rest of them? No wonder Rohini was vexed with him, he thought. A wife should have her own kitchen, fireside, tawa, pot. But he was empty-handed, owning nothing he could not make himself. He could wind a strip of leather around wood to make a catapult but what was that but a boy's plaything? He could pick fadu from trees and form them into a necklace, but she already had an excess of these from him. The little box he had made for her and lined with a strip from his mother's sari was already crammed with such boyish gifts. What she needed was land, house, kitchen, cow, baby, like Mala. Mala's parents had made a poor match with a boy from the neighbouring village. They had built him a hut on their own plot and furnished it with all the implements Mala needed to cook food for him. When Mala became pregnant the boy went to her parents and demanded a cow. She would probably become pregnant every year and the boy would gain more and more of the herd until they had nothing left. She was their only child and the shame would be too much to live with if he deserted her. Should he have married Mala as his mother wanted? He discarded the question hurriedly from his mind. No, he *desired* Rohini, even though she came from a lesser caste. It was her stubbornness which bound him to her, her refusal to put up with his uselessness. He felt it in the silence with which she put his plate of food before him or the silence with which she allowed him to play with her at nights. And when she demanded of him, taking his hand

36

and putting it to her body, she seemed to do so only to expose his weakness. He wanted to move his mouth downwards from her breasts to the space he had never seen and would never see in the darkness of the rice sack. A single moment of taste would do, though, the tiniest splashing on his tongue, but he was afraid to move from her breasts and she did not encourage him by guiding his head downwards. She would only let him spread and close his fingers there, as if his hand were a mere kitchen cloth to soak up spillage.

'So you not fuckie-fuckie the child fully yet?' Kumar said in a tone verging on laughter. Vidia shuddered at Kumar's obsession with hurting women by naming the parts of their bodies. He looked down at his bare feet, regretting that he had befriended the man. 'No shame boy, you tell me nothing I ain't dream already.'

'How you know?' Vidia asked, wondering whether the whole village could also sense his misery and were ridiculing him secretly.

'There is nothing on earth or sky I can't reckon. How much stars come out at night, you know?'

Vidia shook his head.

'Three hundred and seventy-seven thousand, three hundred and nought. Not one more. Not one less. All of them I count. Forty-nine years it take me. I divide the sky in seventy-seven portions. Then the years in seven parts. Each year, over seven years, I count eleven portions, then another eleven, till I finish. Just in case I miss one star and the whole system lop-sided I start again last year to re-count. You know why one more or one less star is disaster?'

'No,' Vidia answered, convinced that Kumar was either mad or crookish in some complicated way.

'Because everything come in seven. Everything multiply in seven. If only one single tiny star appear to make the number three hundred and seventy-seven thousand, three hundred and one, then it is God's sign that the whole world ending soon. Famine and pestilence and woman breeding beast. God does only give slight-slight sign and you got to ransack the universe for it. That's why I now re-counting.'

'But you will dead-out before another forty-nine years how-soever you speed.'

'Ah, that is where you stupid. You think in forty-nine years I ain't work out system? Numbers got magic. I don't have to count one-one no more. I can jump figures.'

'Like fleas,' Vidia retaliated, picking up his water-coconuts to go. 'You reckon yet how much live on your skin and how much die under your fingernail?'

'Boy!' Kumar shrieked, hobbling after him, more concerned about the loss of water-coconuts than Vidia's insults. 'Boy, stop right now or I let go one curse worse than scorpion on your face.'

Vidia continued on his way, agitated by Kumar's reference to his ignorance. He didn't care what spell Kumar put on him. Nothing the old man could do was worse than the shame he suffered. He was convinced the whole village knew that he had not done it properly with Rohini. Why else was everyone so intimate all of a sudden? 'Vidia boy, since you marry you look so haggard. Take it easy boy, take it easy,' one of them called out as he headed for the field at dawn. When he returned at the close of the day another shouted, 'Vidia, why you hurry so? Come in and knock back some liquor, wife will taste more sweet.'

Kumar gave up chasing after him and stood his guard. 'So you don't want my money?' he shouted, 'alright, go. I leave it bury in the ground.' Kumar watched him hesitate then stop. 'Yes, money. Only money can catch Rohini pussy proper,' he said, grinning callously, relishing his control over the boy. 'Unless you want to snap and bruk-up all your life.'

'Why I should believe you have money?' Vidia asked, handing over the water-coconuts. He peered into Kumar's hut. There was nothing to see. Not one plate nor pot. Not one blanket nor shred of clothing.

'I bury everything,' Kumar said, addressing the boy's puzzlement, 'only I left above ground. One day when I dead I will be my own treasure. They will put me in hole since I left no money behind for ghee and pandit and riverside ceremony.'

'So how much money I will get from you?' Vidia insisted, still perplexed by Kumar's motives.

'As much as you can count stars between the Gabreta and Majsaru, as wise people call those areas of the sky.'

'What all this stupidness about stars when is rupee numbers I want,' Vidia groaned.

'One thousand, three hundred and seventy-two,' Kumar answered automatically. 'I bury seven rupees each in one hundred and ninety-six different holes in twenty-eight parts of this village. Seven parts in this yard and the other twenty-one scatter about.' And he picked up a stick and began to draw a diagram on the ground. Vidia examined the marks, unable to make sense of them. The readiness with which Kumar supplied numbers convinced him, though, that the man was telling the truth.

'Ignorance is your name or what?' Kumar taunted. 'This here is Gabreta and this Majsaru, both in seven sections, and this is the triangle showing the pattern of the holes.'

Vidia grew agitated at his inability to follow Kumar's reasoning.

'It is hole you have in your brain,' Kumar said in a deadpan, mocking voice, 'hole so big that even India not have rupee enough to stuff in it.'

Vidia stared at Kumar's head, then reached to pick up a stone. 'One more insult from you and I swear I...'

'Do what?' Kumar interrupted him. 'What can a boy in heat do to a man like me who for seventy-seven years never pine for woman flesh. You lack emptiness, that's why you so wretched. Take your water-coconuts and go, see if I bother. You bring eight anyway, one too many. The lot bound to have sour water in them and worm-jelly.' He turned his back to Vidia and shuffled towards his hut. 'Emptiness is God self,' he said, as if speaking to himself, but loud enough for Vidia to hear. 'That's why I rid everything I own except one piece of cloth for my waist and I bury all my money. I sleep naked-skin on earth. When I wake up I drink water and suck fruit. I save nothing, not even the teeth in my mouth.'

'You lie!' Vidia called after him, drawn into the old man's story. 'From boy you was beggar till now.'

'But what you know about money when a sackful of goat shit more precious than you?' Kumar laughed. 'What you know about woman nipple and tongue? I give up more fuck and treasure than you could ever dream to count.' He entered his hut satisfied that he had conquered the boy's spirit.

For six days Kumar subsisted on the few mangoes that fell to the ground from the only tree in his yard. He was too invalid to pick them, waiting for the wind or the weight of their ripeness to sever them from the branches. Vidia passed his gate with his goats but Kumar would not acknowledge him, squatting before his hut and sucking defiantly on a mango seed. The last mango of the season hung richly from a high branch. Kumar waited patiently for it, noting its growing yellowness, calculating the moment of total hunger. In the mean time he would feed on his own pain. He would outwait the moaning of his stomach as he had for seven decades, as if it were a spoilt child needing to be disciplined by being ignored. Like Vidia. He would not greet the boy nor beg of him the use of his young limbs to climb the tree.

Vidia hurried past the gate resolutely but from the corner of his eye he could see Kumar staring pathetically at the mango as if it were one of his stars he had forgotten to count and which now threatened calamity. He imagined he could hear him whimpering. Six days had elapsed and still the fruit held steadily to the tree. Kumar seemed to be withering fast, the skin slackening even more from his body. The look on his face was one Vidia remembered from childhood when famine ravished the village and the old people sat blankly at the entrances of their huts. They neither cried nor grimaced, just sat there emptily until the wind keeled them over. It was as if someone had knocked over the clay statues of Lord Rama and Lord Krishna from the hearth of his father's house. The villagers fell stiffly and lay forsaken on the ground. The wind blew dust and straw over their faces and flies moved in garlands over them, circling and circling as if making arti to the images of gods.

On the seventh morning Kumar dragged himself to his gate, waiting for Vidia. He curled his body and shivered like a tuft of cowhide caught in wire. Let the sun suck him dry or let him slowly fray in the wind, he would not surrender. 'Aay!' Vidia shouted, shocked at the sight. He rushed into the yard in time to prevent Kumar slumping to the ground. He propped him against the fence and looked around for a puddle of water to wet his mouth or a broad leaf to fan him. 'Kumar man, how come you manage to live like insect all these years?' Vidia asked frantically as he surveyed the dry yard, 'And how you stink!' Kumar's flesh folded stickily around the boy's hands. When he withdrew, flakes of skin were pasted on to them. 'Why you starve yourself so?' Vidia chided, wiping his hands clean on the sides of his trousers, then scrabbling them in a patch of dust to get rid of the smell.

'Starve? What nonsense you talking?' Kumar asked, looking at Vidia with fierce eyes. Now that the boy was in proximity again, he could feel the venom gathering on his tongue like a restorative. 'To be true there are two kinds of starvation,' he said, assuming the calm and patient tone of a teacher. 'There's the starvation you have with Rohini when you dribbling to get into her pokey, then there's starvation proper which is the spirit of India.' He paused and retreated into himself momentarily as if dwelling on Vidia's predicament. 'Come to think of it boy,' he resumed in a voice of false sympathy, 'you must really know what suffering is, eh? Night after night you lying there and her pokey stretch and stretch in circles like someone throw a stone in her. Meanwhile you stay on the bank and scrunch up tight-tight inside yourself. Tell me, what is you?' Vidia looked at Kumar, seeing only the substance of himself. He felt Kumar's emaciation in his own flesh, in the husk between his legs. At least Kumar contained the hurt even though the mango hung like a lantern before his face, showing the cracked earth, the veins of drought that gathered to the side of his mouth then ran down his chin and neck in a cascade of self-mockery. Kumar could so easily beseech him to pick the mango but no! Kumar would rather wait until it fell by itself and the rat, hearing the thud, scrambled from its hole to devour it before he could crawl to retrieve it.

'You is me, what I will be, a blight-up star,' Vidia answered in a moment of perfect understanding of the old man's defiance, 'and the rat will come and take everything away, you and me and everybody.'

'And what will happen to Rohini?' Kumar asked with sudden misgiving. He was moved by Vidia's compassion for him and felt strangely generous, strangely protective. He had mocked him long enough.

'The rat will nibble away at the blight, then nibble away at her and leave infection.'

Kumar shook his head, wanting to retrieve Vidia from his

mood of bleakness, wanting the boy to believe again in prophecy. 'Money is all you dream, money for Rohini so rat don't run off with her. But I lie to you. It is not money or rat-mouth gleaming with gold teeth the child want.'

'What else then?' Vidia asked. 'I is nothing, I own nothing and I grow up to be like you, nothing.'

Kumar picked up a stick and peeled off the bark aimlessly. He flung the flakes as far away from him as he could, appalled by the sight of even drier wood beneath the skin. 'You is not me, you hear, you is not me,' he said quietly. The effort of explaining things to the boy seemed to exhaust him. He slumped against the fence, muttering to himself but working his gums to a froth as if to snuffle the words. 'Listen, boy. I will tell you what you will be. I can prosper you or I can rampage you with disease.'

'Quiet Kumar, save yourself, quiet. Let me fetch you something to eat,' Vidia said, worried again by the quaking of the old man's body.

'No, stay and hear me. I speak no more like this again. Stay.'

'But one more hour in this sun and you dead! Let me go call Ma,' Vidia cried out.

'Stop this stupidness boy! Seventy-seven years I live and you think I will dead out on such a barren morning? I will wait for what I never had, for rain to perfume my skin and the ground splatter with fruit, then softly I will say no, and laugh and expire.'

'But why you want emptiness like that?' Vidia asked, staring into Kumar's mouth as it opened and closed. He suddenly had a vision of Rohini's nipple brushing against Kumar's face, demanding to be pleasured. She would squeeze both breasts together and press them into Kumar's mouth; as his tongue loosened from shackles of lovelessness and struggled to suck, she would withdraw them, the emptiness making him salivate, making him issue out of his infertility. Her naked advances would so easily make Kumar deny the character he had cultivated over his lifetime.

'Look how your mouth mash in, like Rohini pluck out your tongue,' Kumar said tenderly, sensing Vidia's confusion. 'But then you want her to come at you, eh, like some beast? How come you so mousy and don't slap and cuff her like a man till she bow down in sufferation?' Vidia looked away, unable to answer. 'One-two blows now and then good for woman, so it says in the scriptures.'

'You promise me money,' Vidia said pathetically.

Kumar, having loosed him to his own despair, spooled him back. 'Plenty money,' he assured the boy, 'and when you are full-handed, go far away. Flee to some other land where food plenty, where Rohini belly yield every year and you grow your own colony. Five acres and cow and wife and children.'

'You talking mad again man. When you will stop poke fun and prophesy true thing?'

'But it is so I dream,' Kumar said, pressing his palms with great effort into the earth to straighten his body. He crossed his legs and sat upright before the boy like a famined Buddha. The slightest wind threatened to tilt him but when Vidia went to steady him, he pushed him away. 'Listen,' he snapped, 'sit quiet and learn, or go. Which you want?' Vidia sat down reluctantly as Kumar envisioned a land that was slowly drying up as each year passed. Cracks opened up and people cried, how their stomachs burned, and some took up machetes and chopped each other into fire-wood, but there was still no food in the pot howsoever they rampaged. Village against village, city against city, caste against caste, and still not one grain of corn to feed even a Brahmin. Hindu and Sikh and Mohammedan all formed one tormented body like Lord Shiva with many hands, each holding weaponry, each reaching to slice off the other. 'Even a small boy like you will grow old and naked-skin overnight. All the suffering which normally spread over a lifetime will thicken in you in seven days. First your sockets loosen and your eye slip inwards to witness your own emptying. Then your tongue reach out like bird-lime branch but nothing catch. Your bowels stretch in boa-mouth yawn and bite into your belly-lining. For three more days you nourish on yourself, muscle, hair, scum, till day seven when British soldiers come in braid and buttons.'

'Man, Kumar, stop your mad mouth,' Vidia said, getting up and going to fetch his Ma. 'Don't dead before I come back,' he pleaded, surveying the yard for tell-tale bumps or broken earth.

'British!' he shouted, catching hold of Vidia's legs and pulling him to the ground with unexpected strength. 'British come

44

hauling a boar more huge that if you flatten it against the sky you block out Gabreta – the bristles alone poke out two-three stars in Majsaru. Boar that carry enough flesh to feed God mouth, but they butcher it and build fort and barrack around it to keep you and we from what belong to all-body. So go boy! Story done! No more India unless you want stay and suck bone.'

'Vidia not enough,' Rohini cursed under her breath as she patted fresh mud over the cracks in the hut. There seemed no end to work, all of which she had to do now that a mysterious illness had incapacitated Droopatie. 'Oh God how my elbow-bone hurt today,' Droopatie moaned, rubbing her flesh in exaggerated gestures. 'One day girl, when you get old like me, you will be so glad to have dutiful daughter-in-law.' She forced her eyes to water as if lamenting her loss of authority. 'Me too frail even to roll roti.' She stared at her hands in self-pity then hobbled outside to catch the morning sun. 'You mustn't mind, you hear,' she called out from the verandah. 'Soon dead I will dead and then house and all in it will pass to Vidia and you.'

'What I want with bruk-down leaning place like this,' Rohini muttered to herself, 'big-big world outside, tall stone houses and courtyards with fountains and carriages rolling down wide streets.' The recruiter had described Calcutta's buildings of red sandstone and tile-mosaics, holding up pictures of domed temples and dwellings embellished with vaults, columns, architraves.

'British people them come and clear away all we mud and bamboo huts and put up thing like this,' he said proudly, showing them a drawing of the Governor's residence – a massive building surrounded by colonnades, its arches enriched with white marble and coloured stones.

'And next to Governor palace is depot where ship waiting to take you to Guiana once you agree to recruit.'

'If you set foot in this spot again,' the village-elder threatened, 'it is dog and mad bull I set on you, you hear? Last time you came you bring gun and now you fire up people head with foolish word. Go before you get arrest for trespass and making distress!'

'This land here no more belong to Indians,' the recruiter

retaliated, putting the pictures back into his sack, 'and you got no power to shift me, not even with one battalion of Indian police. Everything own by British and I am agent of British.'

'British!' the elder shouted, searching the ground for a stick to drive him away. 'Come close, let me British your backside!'

'I warning all of you,' the recruiter said looking around calmly, 'don't listen to this foolish man. He know nothing but how to lash buffalo and reap rice. He is hignorant peasant and he never see city and he don't understand one thing about history or what going on now. I tell you, British coming and all-you will scoot.'

'But what we do British that they want take we land?' someone asked. 'Plus by Law we own the land. Law will stand up for us, no?'

'Law is British now, I am telling you,' the recruiter pleaded as if moved by compassion for their simplicity, 'ever since Muslim cause strife. Less than one hundred miles from here, over river yonder, war going on, Muslim slaughtering and British fighting back, killing everybody, they don't care who is sow-keeper from Hindu, who Brahmin from hill-coolie. Once you is brown, is pow! pow! Gunshot bore hole in you and bayonet like plough in your arse.'

The elder raised his stick and summoned some men to chase the recruiter from the village compound, but no one stirred. 'Let the man speak,' a voice called out timidly and a murmur of approval sustained it.

'Who dare disobey?' the elder said in a soft voice, casting a sinister eye on the villagers. 'He will speak if me and me alone permit.' The very fact that he had to remind them of his authority unhinged him momentarily.

'Let the man speak,' the same voice urged, this time more emphatic as if emboldened by the elder's lapse of self-confidence. The crowd stirred and others broke the silence. 'Madness!' one old man cried out. 'All-you will bring famine in this village. Famine, I tell you, and God damn your children and children-children for disobeying Brahmin! Madness!' He emerged from the body of people and fell before the elder, begging forgiveness. Others followed, forming a clump of abjectness at his feet.

'Let the man speak,' the voice insisted, refusing to be cowed even though its anonymity was compromised by a diminished crowd. If discovered, a severe beating was certain, or worse, once the recruiter left and normality returned.

'British free nigger slaves long ago but you people beyond British salvation!' the recruiter said, siding with the handful of surly peasants who stood apart from the elder. 'And let me tell you something else,' he said, turning to challenge the elder. 'If anyone but raise hand or even scowl at British agent, then it is mayhem let loose in this mangy-bitch village. What British do to them Muslim rebels – hang, stab, chop, debowel – is nothing what they will do to whoever only touch British agent.' He spoke calmly, barely raising his voice even when detailing the dismemberment which awaited them. They were convinced by the lack of passion in his voice. They looked upon him in mournful silence, awaiting instruction. 'First, kill all the Muslims in this village,' he said, confident that his edict would be warmly received by the backward Hindus. 'And wherever you can find them,' he added, to whet their appetites for a wider arena of violence. 'Slaughter the men and feed them to the village pigs then force that same pig-meat, uncooked, down their wives' and children's mouths.'

'Suppose we stuff it in Muslim woman pokey-hole?' the anonymous voice asked, speaking their secret lust.

'Mouth or pokey-hole or arse-hole, or puncture she belly and bore new hole, it is all one to me,' the recruiter replied in a deadpan manner knowing that his authority over them lay in being unexcited by the prospect of rape. He paused to let them savour the promise of murdering their neighbours and looting their property as their fathers and forebears had done for centuries upon the slightest pretext. Afterwards they would rinse the slaughter from their limbs and their booty of bracelets, nose-rings, brass lotas, in the same village ponds they took their cattle to, then go home to light devotional fires before clay gods.

'No war will fight in my village,' the elder protested, breaking the calm of their fantasies, drawing them back to the reality of their poverty. 'Long-standing peace in this place, everybody got work to do, whether Muslim or Hindu, whether one make pot and one keep swine and one name the born. It is either you work or else you cause strife and starve.'

'And what work you conduct that make you chief?' the recruiter asked, smiling maliciously at the elder, then turning to the assembly in an appeal for support.

'I own, I don't labour,' the elder replied dismissively, 'and I don't take question from servants like you.'

'And how come you own when you don't work to own?' the recruiter persisted. 'You mean to say you thief from other people?'

'Ranjit,' the elder barked, looking down at his feet, and a man, naked but for a strip of jute fastened around his waist, separated from the crowd and stood up. He held a cutlass in his hand, his only possession. 'Ranjit, how much grain you owe me?'

'Seven-eight headload, sah.' His face was chipped with age and worry but he managed a gay smile. 'And twelve rupees,' he added brushing away with the tip of his cutlass two flies that had settled to mate on his leg.

'Ranjit, from today all your debts are forgiven. You owe me nothing. You are a free man.'

'Thank you, thank you, sah.' Ranjit fell to the ground and bowed to the elder. He didn't understand what had been said to him but he still grovelled. If the elder had tripled the sum Ranjit would have accepted the calculation and gladly kissed his feet. As long as he was in debt, whatever the size, he had a place in the affections and consideration of his superior.

'Ranjit, if I command you to kill this Christian outcaste what you would do?'

'Kill, sah,' Ranjit answered automatically, looking up with a perplexed expression as if the elder would believe otherwise.

'And how you will kill?' the elder asked, staring hard at the recruiter, then at the group of villagers who stood apart. The knot of surliness loosened under the steadiness of his gaze. They shifted uncertainly, threatening to expose the one among them who had first dared to question his authority.

'Chop, sah.'

'Chop where?'

'Neck, sah.'

'Ranjit, each year when I sacrifice a lamb for the village who do the ceremony?'

'Me, sah.'

'Tell this Christian how you perform your duty.'

'I tie it up, front foot and back foot. I beat it hard with bamboo stick to make the flesh soft. I slit the neck. I hang it up to bleed. I skin it. I scoop out the guts. I garland it with hibiscus.'

'I don't bleat, I am British agent,' the recruiter said, struggling to maintain courage as he gathered his bag and prepared to go. When he was a comfortable distance from them but within earshot he threatened to report them as Muslim sympathisers. 'Wait till British come. We wipe out all your backwardness and slavery and plant new government. Young people who learn talk English and show manners will take over and elders like you will be put to work to grease British bullets in pig-fat.'

Rohini churned the milk that had clabbered overnight, then put it on the mud stove to boil. In the meantime she pounded some rice in a stone cup and peeled onions and potatoes in preparation for their afternoon meal. When she finished in the kitchen other tasks beckoned. She made cow-dung cakes for the fire. She tightened the odd rope that had slackened in the hammock. She swept up scraps of corn cobs and chaff. She watered the garden of chilli peppers and egg-plants. Droopatie had left a bundle of her clothing which needed mending. An hour before Vidia and Harilall, his father, came home she began to cook. After eating the father rested and it was her job to massage his neck and back. He lay half-naked before her. At first she was afraid of being left alone with him in the bedroom but slowly she grew to enjoy her power over him and the intimacy with which she probed his flesh. The rankness of cattle and stagnant water emanated from his body. Sometimes he would turn over and command her to rub his belly and thighs. Droopatie would often interrupt them, coming into the bedroom with a bowl of cherries to offer him, but really to investigate the reason for their silence.

Rohini had never seen Vidia naked but she knew his body and how to arouse it from these sessions with his father. As they lay under the rice bag she knew how to press and slide her fingers along Vidia's chest or to touch him almost accidentally on his thighs then remove her hand in a show of apology and shame. As she made love to him she remembered how his father had slackened when she touched him in a certain way. Vidia was always more nervous, his limbs immaturely taut and his body on the edge of convulsion. He smelt like a boy, she thought, a sticky freshness like the milk of a newly bled tree. She preferred the coarseness of his father's skin, its mat of hairs which, when

51

ruffled, gave off an odour of dust, saltpetre, over-ripe limes, cloves – each smell different from day to day.

'Let we leave this pit and go Guiana with British,' Rohini suggested to Vidia on one of the few occasions they could converse. His parents had gone to a meeting summoned by the elder, leaving the two of them to shell peas.

'But who will look after goat and cow?' Vidia asked.

She looked up from the bowl and confronted his small, timid face. She had let him enter her the night before but he grew sweaty too quickly, then spent, leaving her with his limp cry ringing annoyingly in her ears. Better she had put a bouquet of pig bristles inside her, she thought. 'Vidia, you can't be a man in this place. No money here.' As expected, he quickened with hurt. It was so easy to manipulate him, unlike his father who, even though he slouched in pleasure under her massage, would stiffen at any moment and dismiss her to the kitchen with a knowing grunt. 'How you expect to live without money? How you expect to support children? The barber, the washerman, the bangle-seller, the drain-cleaner, the carpenter – all of them want payment or else the place ruin, latrine choke up, people eat weed or hog. As to Brahmin he will not say prayer except for four yards cloth, even though the dead body swelling and stinking up the whole village whilst waiting for him to commence ceremony. Then you got to bribe headman and policeman and rentman with corn or pulse, or else misery they make for you.'

'Shut your mouth,' Vidia rebuked her, raising his hand as if to hit her as he had seen his father do when his mother spoke aggressively. His gesture of authority pleased her as much as it startled him.

'But Vidia,' she said, gently lowering her eyes to the bowl of peas, 'I only want sweetmeat for your mouth and to lie for you all day in feather-bed.'

'You can't be happy without money?' he asked in desperation.

'It is not money,' she said, raising her hand and stroking his face submissively. 'Recruiter say Guiana have plenty land, you can turn man and own so much you can't see the fencing how it is so far in front. And if you kick topsoil and one-two stones, gold greet your eye. Why stay here? You wake up, you eat, you go and mind cattle, you come back home, you sleep, till you dead one day with diarrhoea or worry over debt. Recruiter say outside have plenty action, people live in city and wear bright clothes and walk avenue and eat with spoon and fight war. I want fight war, Vidia, big-big war, not spend all day and the next day killing weevil in a bowl of peas.'

'Kumar pledge me plenty rupee,' Vidia offered hesitantly, 'and I can buy over his land and build.'

She looked up and sniggered.

'Why you laughing?' he asked, hurt by her sudden disrespect.

She sniggered again.

'Why you laughing?' He wanted to hit her. 'You forget your place or what?'

She said nothing, staring into the bowl, massaging a few tiny peas between her fingertips in self-absorption. She was doomed to his insufficiency. Kumar abused him with promises and in return Vidia served him, supplying fruit to the dying man. Every day on his way to the savannah he emptied his pockets of figs stolen from his mother's kitchen. In return Kumar gave him small portions of dust in different hues in which he had dropped pieces of mango leaf. 'Sprinkle this blue one on her before you enter,' or 'mix this red one with goat-milk and make paste and rub it inside her slow,' he commanded the boy, teaching him a special Sanskrit mantra to recite to bring out the magical properties of the dust. Ignorant boy! She must get out, if only she could leave him. But it was *she* who had hurried to marry him. Better to have listened to her mother and stayed single for a little longer. She and Finee could have followed the recruiter to Calcutta there and then and put their thumb-prints to the paper he said would give them priority berth to Guiana. Instead each night she lay open-eyed whilst Vidia scratched and dug and made silly little cooing noises. She suffered the pastes and potions and mutterings in Sanskrit. If she closed her eyes she could smell Kumar and almost feel his hand plying her body, flaking and issuing within her. She kept them open to remind herself that she was under the rice bag with Vidia. At least he was young and obedient and devoted to her. A thousand families would gladly make match with their daughters. It was only six months since their marriage – perhaps she should give him more time to escape his parents. Yes, she was being nasty and selfish, thinking only of what *she* wanted, and how soon, whilst neglecting her duties to her mother-in-law. Tomorrow she would darn Droopatie's clothes properly instead of making slack, untidy stitches. She would stop cursing in the cup of milk before giving it to her. She would show willingness to everyone, even Kumar. He was old and loveless. No woman had ever massaged his body. No woman had even put her tongue in his mouth or raged as he entered her. She suspected Kumar's delight when Vidia rubbed between her thighs and the following day reported all the details of her responses: the sudden burning that made her want to scream or the pieces of grit that bruised and drew blood. But she would not deny Kumar his pleasure with her. The same with Vidia's father. Men worked hard only to end up with belly-wind like Kumar, or a scowling fat clumsy wife like Droopatie who had long forgotten, once she bore the children, how to give love to her husband. Finee too, her own mother, who had treated Jagnat only as a pair of hands to plough. As long as he brought home food she would put up with his crippled condition. Finee still would not arouse Jagnat, letting him sleep beside her half-naked body as adequate reward. If only Jagnat had lived to see her, Rohini, marry and have sex. She would have satisfied him somehow, as she did Kumar, and her father-in-law. That's all men wanted – a little desperation in their heads, a little exhaustion afterwards. She was young. She could give and give and still remain dutifully fresh for Vidia.

'How much I have to give to get passage to Guiana?' In the confusion following the recruiter's visit Rohini had escaped Droopatie's watchfulness, running a quarter of a mile to catch up with him.

'How much you get?' he barked, still smarting from the elder's humiliation of him.

'One rupee,' Rohini answered breathlessly.

'One rupee and your scunt more like,' he said, chuckling to himself. In her eagerness to pursue him she had run out wearing her house clothes, forgetting to bring her shawl. She drew the folds of her blouse closer to her but her breasts still felt exposed.

'One rupee and your scunt,' he repeated, this time without laughter, 'can take you to Guiana. And back. Well? What you say?' His eyes swept her body, alighting on a small brown mole on her neck like an aroused nipple.

'But I is a married woman,' she said. The words came automatically and foolishly from her mouth.

'Married scunt is sweetest,' he whispered, putting down his sack and making to unbuckle his belt. She turned and hurried from him. 'Alright, alright, you can keep the rupee!' he shouted after her, gratified when she seemed to hesitate.

Rohini entered the cow pen stealthily even though Vidia and his parents, along with most of the villagers, had gone to witness the destruction of the Muslims. She could smell the smoke from the Muslim compound which lay a few hundred yards outside the village. An occasional scream rose above the murmur of voices. A woman, it sounded like this time. Perhaps they were dragging her to the ditch to be drowned. Still, it was for the best. What did she, Rohini, have to do with Muslim and British? Besides, who really knew why people killed? 'War break out for true and if British come here and find Muslim, everybody done for. So we finish them first and find favour with British.' So Droopatie had explained it to her, all excited, as if it was the first time in her life she was talking sense. At least when the fire died and everybody was bathed clean of blood, she and Vidia could board the boat for Guiana. The British surely would be glad to ferry them and not charge one rupee. Plus she could sell her bangle for five rupees, and the nine Vidia got for his dowry made fourteen, which they could take to Guiana as savings. Another scream disturbed her reckoning, this time unending, as if the flesh was being lanced in several small places to let out bad blood. She poured the bucket of poison into the drinking trough, the kumari seeds Finee had given her to stop her womb, crushed with nin leaves and boiled in water, with a sprinkling of Kumar's dust added just for spite. She had concocted the mixture earlier in the day whilst Droopatie slept, all the time justifying what had to be done to release her from the village. The killing of the cow was unthinkable, which is why she would do it. The sudden death of the animal would be taken as a curse on the family. Why else would the gods mark them out like this? The initial pity of neighbours would give way to gloating at their downfall. Gossip would arise, she calculated, the villagers speculation on the evil Vidia's family had performed in their previous lives. With luck they would single out Droopatie for some particularly nasty deed. But what? Meanness wasn't sufficient – she had enough of that in the present life, as did everybody else. Adultery? Rohini looked upon the sleeping woman, at the spittle that had dried at the corners of her mouth, a darkening cake that attracted flies. Could Droopatie in her past life have been so different from the nauseous heap she was now that many men sinned with her? No, it couldn't be so. Something more shameful, more appropriate to her gross body, something to do with… goats! She giggled to herself, feeding more berries into the pot. Anyway, whatever it was, the villagers' gloating would turn into a belief that the curse was contagious. The family would be shunned as outcasts. They would *have* to leave and settle elsewhere. They would become paupers since no one would dare buy their house and land. It was then that Rohini could insist that Vidia move to Guiana to earn money to support his parents. As to the gods, well, she would have left them behind when they reached the new land at the other side of the earth. The gods let Muslims be butchered, so what was a mere cow? Besides, the British had other gods. And more powerful, she reasoned, for the recruiter had told them that all of India was only a fraction of British wealth, a copper bangle among white diamonds, roughly crafted, distressingly brown.

'But what will happen to me?' Finee sobbed. 'When you go Guiana the British will come and take me in pig pen.' Vidia fell silent. He waited for Rohini to speak.

'You only exaggerate,' Rohini said, knowing her mother's tricks.

Finee began to wail. 'Just because I lose most of my teeth so my cheeks drop don't mean I will escape British attention. No man in the village yet wink at me since Jagnat dead, but British different. They is foreign. They is far from home. Just because Rohini breasts prime and brazen don't make her alone qualify for massacre. Look what happen to Rashida,' Finee cried out, addressing Vidia. 'You been there. I see you watching what happen to Rashida.'

Vidia scanned the hut, trying to alight on some neutral object which would occupy his attention.

'A woman who harm nobody. From the time she born she clean latrine for a living. Till the smell marry into her skin, flies follow her everywhere like if they is her own children. But still, and even with the smallpox that pit her face, what all-you do?' Finee stopped crying and looked accusingly at Vidia.

'What all-you do?' Rohini demanded, suddenly fascinated by Vidia's potential. Silence had sealed the village since the massacre. She was curious for days but Droopatie rebuked her for her questions. Now she would bully the truth from Vidia.

'I only went to see the fire,' he said childishly.

'See the fire? See the fire?' Finee sneered. 'You mean see this!' And in seeming grief for Rashida's fate she ripped off her clothes and stood naked before them. Before they could recover she worked up a shuddering of her body and stumbled forward as if to collapse. Another wail escaped her mouth. 'Shut up! Shut up!' Rohini screamed, unwrapping the shawl from her shoulders to cover Finee. But Finee pushed her hand away and fell defiantly to the ground. Let them dare go to Guiana and leave her in this state, just let them! For all Rohini's hardness, she, Finee, was still Ma. She would curse and plead and pretend madness and call Lord Krishna's name until duty made Rohini stay. She taught the girl to grow brash as any man and not to take licks and bad sex from any man but she never taught her to sin. Lord Krishna be her witness, make her blind and crippled if she lied, but she never taught Rohini to sin. And if Rohini went to Guiana and left her, then Rohini would be sinning.

'You profit from Rashida misery,' Rohini shouted at her, pointing to two pots that Finee had helped herself to from Rashida's kitchen whilst the men were busy with her. 'You only crying because you didn't thief some more!' Finee refused to be stilled by guilt, continuing her antics. 'Vidia, don't just stand there stupidy-stupidy! Tell her you will send gold from Guiana. Make her stop cry. Tell her you will come back soon in two-three season with plenty money.'

Vidia did nothing. He was not listening to Rohini. He was staring at Finee's breasts – one had shrunk back into itself and flattened out into the head of a spindle, or the eye of a blighted star. A line of hair originating under one nipple ran the length of her chest and disappeared into the hole of her navel. Another line of hair started up and grew into a messy ant-hill around her thighs. It was the first time he had seen a woman so completely naked. So this was what he cursed for in all the months of marriage with Rohini – ants; what he was preparing to leave everything behind for. He wanted to call out to his parents, boyishly, as he once could before taking a wife. He wanted to feel his mother's hand patting oil into his hair, reminding him of how small and promising he was. But Finee would not let him, shuddering on the ground and pleading to him, as Rashida had done before his father and some other men finished her off.

PART II

KAMPTA

Vidia emptied his jars and arranged the coins in seven piles according to their denomination. Seven was his lucky number. He was born in the seventh month of 1836. There were seven in his family: his parents, four girls and himself. And it was in 1857 (the sum of the numbers was divisible by seven) that he and Rohini set off for Calcutta and the voyage across the Atlantic.

In the depot awaiting shipment, whiteman had held up a holy book called the Bible and told them in Hindi how English god made the universe in seven days. He marvelled at how whiteman could speak their language so nicely, better than he did. It made him feel ashamed, tongue-tied and from an obscure village. First sky, then sea, then fowl, then cow, then man, then woman, and on the seventh day God finished and rested, but no, not Vidia! Only nigger people slept when there was so much work to do, so much riches to be got by piece-work or day-wage, however buckra boss chose to pay, and for chopping, weeding, manuring, pan-boiling and seven hundred other tasks each giving seven cents or seventy cents. In Plantation Albion you could work till you dropped. Nigger people turned Christian so they could mimic English god and laze on Sunday, but he, Vidia, was on the hunt for job, beseeching Gladstone, the manager, to let him weed his yard, even if the manager wouldn't pay, except for a sackful of star-apples which he could sell for a dollar or change for a hen which would yield one egg a day, selling at five cents each, thirty-five cents a week profit. Money was everywhere, even in fowl-belly and fowl-battie, he only had to get at it. And if you lent it out, money could breed money, a miracle – even though metal, each coin could bring forth other coins, like how a man could multiply himself into seven children.

The unexpected analogy stung him and he fell silent. Although she was out of sight he could feel Rohini's accusatory presence. She was in the yard scrubbing pots. Eveningtime like now, she should be cleaning their children to send them to bed. But there were none. What went wrong and whose fault was it? Perhaps it was Kumar's curse upon them. He had died a mere year or so after Vidia had torn a piece from his mother's special sari. And Kumar, who had promised to show him the secret burial places which contained rupees, never did so. With the rest of the villagers, he had dug up Kumar's yard but found nothing. For nights on end Vidia studied the configuration of stars, trying to discover some pattern which resembled the positioning of trees or stones on the land, marking the places where Kumar hid his money, but he could not understand Kumar's ways of thinking. That was the eternal problem – his ignorance of everything. The tall stone buildings in Calcutta – who had put them up and how? The ship docked, waiting to take them to Guiana – how could human beings design such a structure? How did it float even though it looked as big in size as his village? Everything buckra people were involved in had an aspect of magic to it and what was he but a peasant without talent? He knew nothing, only how to mind cow and goat, how to plant papaya and watch it change colour from green to yellow to ochre, then when the moment was perfect, pick it for Rohini's mouth.

'Plantation Albion not enough,' Rohini fretted as she scrubbed pots and prepared to cook. Waterfrogs croaked like anxious old men cracking and re-cracking their knuckles. Fireflies massed at the pond behind the row of huts, illuminating the surface for no apparent reason. All evening they scratched themselves alight, but the dampness of the air overcame them and they fell into the water to die.

In the early months, at harvest time, she would join the gathering of children at the dam to watch the foreman pour kerosene into a trough running through a patch of cane. He struck a match, the cane trash kindled and the fields soon blazed. The heat reached a flock of doves nesting in the cane and they scattered upward in a cloud of cinder, leaving their young behind.

That was the best time to hunt: the children let loose their slingshots and several birds fell. The fire would roast them thoroughly, and when it was out, the feasting would begin. The cruelty of such scenes used to distress her but she soon grew accustomed to the rituals of cane: fire consuming the trash to make the cane easier to harvest; killing scorpions and snakes to make it safer to work; cooking birdmeat to fill their bellies. The soil was manured, the cane was planted, the fields were weeded, the cane was harvested, and then the cycle of nurturing and killing began again. The factory's machinery was never idle, crushing, boiling, fermenting, distilling, making sugar and rum, molasses and bagasse. Boat-loads of new coolies arrived to clear new fields or to replace those who succumbed to diseases. Many of them died rapidly of the same epidemics, but there was no shortage of ships from India to replenish the work gangs.

She spent the first year in Guiana in a state of exhilaration. She gave herself completely to her domestic tasks, finding time, too, to work in the manager's kitchen, bringing in her own small sum of money to add to Vidia's wages. At the end of each week she sat with him as he counted and re-counted their earnings, organising the coins into separate piles: one to be sent back to India for Finee, the second for his parents, the third for the week's food, the last to be buried under the calabash tree as savings. At the end of five years, when Gladstone would reward him for his service with a free plot of land, he would have accumulated enough to buy wood to build their first home.

'You can wait that long? Five years is long you know?' he asked anxiously, wishing he could make speedier progress by finding extra work to do on the estate, if only the day was twice as long, and the night twice as short. Already he had measured his period of sleep, cutting it down from seven to six to five hours. Five hours affected him though: he barely had strength to chew the food she brought to him in the evening, so he swallowed it in lumps – this gave him belly-ache the next day but he ground his teeth and bore it, for there was a wealth of cane to be cut and if he didn't, the rest of the gang would earn his share and overtake him in possessions. Moreover, he couldn't please her in that state for he collapsed and slept as soon as he lay on the blanket beside her.

65

No, he would give himself two extra hours on Sunday, to count his money correctly and to make her a baby. She could have the baby on a Sunday – work was slack then because Gladstone, being a Christian, limited it. Even if he wanted to work the two extra hours he would have to do it illegally, in the nearby village where the niggers would pay him in corn, or strips of sheepskin, to help clear pond and canal. But what would happen if Gladstone found out, the niggers being so lazy and yet so envious they could easily tell on him? Licks! One month in jail for breaking the contract of his indenture. He didn't mind the licks, even the shame of it, because no one ever beat him but his Pa; and licks healed soon-soon. But not jail! One month without wages! Rohini would have to survive on his savings! The jar would be half empty, worms might as well eat the rest. He might as well die and be buried in the ground and spare the money by giving over his body to the worms.

'Five years will go quick-quick,' she said, wanting to relieve his sudden gloom, 'I can wait ten years if you ask me.'

'Ten years? True? You can live ten years in here?' It was a single room in a sequence of rooms, and she could barely rest: the walls were so thin she could hear every grunt and scratch. When rain fell it dripped through holes in the troolie roof, so they had to huddle for days in one small corner, sharing it with ant and cockroach and centipede. The rain swelled the trough outside the logie which served as an open toilet and refuse dump for every-one; it overflowed, flooding the yards with worms fat and pink as prawns.

'Ten years. Twenty even,' she lied, listening supportively as he outlined plans for their future. Afterwards, in bed, she suc-cumbed to him, letting him vent his ambitions, each novel sensation or manoeuvre marking a further distancing from India and from the past. She was nineteen now, a wife with no one to shackle her. Without Droopatie, Vidia was even more unpro-tected, even more obedient to her moods. She knew there was a shortage of women on the plantation, that many of his fellow cane cutters would scheme with money to bribe her, or with poison to kill him, if only she consented to it. But what could she gain by them, these uncouth coolies who would throw a few coppers her way and expect to devour her in return, then when she had grown shabby and exhausted, put her out to work for other men? She had avoided them from the time they were shepherded on to the ship in Calcutta, each man squeezing against the next at the narrow hatchways, trying to get below quickly to find the best berth. They had with them all their belongings – lengths of cloth, knives, glass mirrors, brass pots, crude bracelets and coins secreted in the hem of their dhotis, in the lining of their blankets, in their stomachs. She fancied she could tell who had swallowed their wealth for safety – in calm weather they sat on deck with a pleasing look, as if listening to the jewellery jingling in their bellies; when the sea was distressed they clenched their mouths, swallowing and re-swallowing whilst all around other coolies abandoned their stomachs, colouring the deck with massala, tumeric and dhall. The recruiter had promised romance, comparing it to the story of Lord Bharrat's journey to Dandaka forest to meet his bride, but in the three long months to Guiana and the two long years following, she met only with the sickness of greed. That was all there was, though, and she might as well find a way of profiting from it. What else could she do, except return to India, to Droopatie's clutch? Here at least she could flatter men or stir them into rage by a mere glance. She could make them forget their sun-baked, blistered faces or the jigger eating away their feet. All they wanted was to grow frantic inside her. Although she would not dream of rejecting Vidia for such men, she still tormented him with the prospect of betrayal. She rubbed oils into her skin to keep it fresh and scented. She massaged her breasts and nipples, as Finee had taught her, to encourage growth. Miriam, the nigger maid in Mr Gladstone's house, showed her how to make curls in her hair, like the whiteladies in the photographs decorating Mr Gladstone's chamber. Miriam gave her pieces of bright African cloth with which to make headbands. By these means she would goad Vidia into achievement. Why should she walk barefooted all her life with nothing but plain cotton to decorate her body? In exchange for his labour she would maintain her body and make children for him, not many... one boy, perhaps another, then she would stop before growing misshapen and outworn.

So why, Rohini brooded as she dabbed oil on the tawa, why was their room still empty after two years? Month succeeded month, gladness hardened and bruised within, her belly soaked up his milk, her breasts stretched in expectancy... but these were only false announcements of child. Month succeeded month, one jar filled up, then another, and was corked tight, and was buried under compact ground but all the time her body was slackening and emptying. They called in pandit to pray but there was still no baby, and Miriam give her bush potions but they might as well be Kumar's doing for they all failed.

It was Kumar who kept awakening her to the guilt of her barrenness. When Vidia had done his counting and settled into bed she made excuses to delay joining him, remembering suddenly some task in the kitchen which she had neglected to complete. She was afraid to sleep for one dream in particular recurred to humiliate her. Lord Rama was leading her through a throng of worshippers, making her pause to allow women to garland her. The air was thick with incense pluming from their mouths. They pressed against her as if to deny her breath and deafen her with their chanting. She felt on the point of collapse when a thousand hands reached to raise her, carrying her as if she were on a bier towards a platform which held two thrones, one for Lord Rama, one for His bride. She struggled to escape, summoning Finee to help her but Finee chided her instead for her ingratitude. They deposited her on a platform before a throne embellished with more stones than all of Kumar's stars and a thousand voices urged her to sit, but she would not, ashamed of her simplicity and peasant's clothing. The moles on her face and neck, which she used to pride as ornaments of beauty, became magnified in her own sight. The more they gazed upon her, the more coarse she became, her blemishes evident to all. Lord Rama stood before her, His hands raised over her head in an attitude of benediction. Her eyes fixed on the bangles of light around His wrist, which blinded her to her own appearance, but when she was about to yield to His forgiveness, He suddenly slapped her across the mouth, churlishly, like an ordinary bully. The chanting and adulation stopped. She reeled back and fell to the ground. When she recovered and looked out, the worshippers had vanished. Only Lord Rama remained, radiant and ordinary. He reached down gently, as if to comfort her, but when she raised her face He slapped her again, drawing blood. The light cracked on His face so that she saw herself in so many fragments bound only by a cord of pain. The edges of broken light sought to cut the cord and shatter her irretrievably. She called out to Finee but no one answered. She scrambled away from His feet as she had done when the recruiter tried to gather her up from the ground, and she fell from the platform into a garden of stones, where Kumar waited, dying, a slick of venom at the side of his mouth. 'Chamar crab-louse,' he cursed, accusing her of taking Vidia from him. 'Nasty-pokey nimakarram bitch!' She ran blindly from him, following the sound of her feet, and she fell into a trough, into a temple of bone, into a white space bound by arches and spirals and columns. It was Kumar's boar, she knew instantly, the stomach of which had been cut open and ransacked; the British seeking nothing but the thrill of degradation, scattering its monumental bones like so many ransacked mosques they had seen in Calcutta, on the way to the emigrants' depot.

'Is because I kill the cow that we get no baby,' Rohini confessed to Vidia on the anniversary of their second year on Plantation Albion. It earned her her first beating from him. She could have moved out and found shelter in Gladstone's house. He seemed moved by her bruises and offered to keep her in his protection for a while. He ordered Miriam to fetch a bowl of warm water and a clean flannel. He sat and watched as Miriam dabbed it on her cheeks which had taken the brunt of Vidia's passion. It was his kindness more than the hurt which made her cry. In her two years of working in his house she had been terrified of him, not daring to remain in a room if he walked in as she was dusting and polishing. He barely paused to say a word to her in all that time, keeping his authority by seeming to ignore her. Now he acknowledged her in an unexpected way, threatening to punish Vidia on her behalf, as her father would have done if he were in Guiana. But Jagnat was dead, and Vidia was her husband, so she must return to him, in spite of the beating which, after all, was only what she deserved; it was only right that Vidia should behave badly for any wife who removed a man from his mother must meet punishment. When she thought of it she was glad he hit her because it proved he had his own will, even though it was not as big and important as Gladstone's who was in charge of more than a wife, but nine-ten hundred coolies, and the mules that pulled the punts to the factory.

Miriam stood at the doorway and muttered – the low suspicious growl of a guard dog – until Gladstone released Rohini into her custody. 'Why you complain to Massa?' she chided, sitting Rohini down in the kitchen before her. 'Only tribulation you will bring on my head.' She went outside, scrabbled around the garden and came back with a handful of leaves. She crushed them into a saucepan. When they were boiled she reached into her bosom, pulled out a handkerchief and shook it violently as if to rid it of scraps of insects which, in curiosity, had wandered on to her chest. Rohini closed her eyes to stop her imagining nasty things about Miriam; Miriam who had taken pity on her malnourished body from the moment she entered Gladstone's house, feeding her with roast plantains or making sure she did only the lightest of work. Still, Vidia's judgement on the niggers stayed with her – they were lazy and ignorant people, living only for their bellies and the day; their huts stank of unwashed children. Miriam dipped her handkerchief in the froth that formed on the boiling water and applied it to Rohini's face, but she recoiled from her. 'Don't frighten. It won't sting or pain,' Miriam assured her, mistaking her attitude.

'What nastiness you get in the handkerchief?' Rohini demanded.

'Ssh child, is only medicine that will heal you in no time,' Miriam answered, innocent of Rohini's spitefulness, 'beatings is we business.' She grasped the back of Rohini's head and held it forcefully in her large palm whilst rubbing the handkerchief around her face. 'Move again and one slap I give you worse than Vidia,' she said in mock warning. 'You know how many times I take lash in my life?' she asked Rohini as if to console her with solidarity. Rohini shook her head, pressing her lips together to prevent any of the liquid entering her mouth. She must have appeared a ludicrous sight for Miriam stood back and burst into laughter. 'A few blows from Vidia and look at you! Why you screw your mouth so as if it empty of teeth? He break off some in truth? Open up let me examine you.' She made to prise apart Rohini's lips and laughed again when she sought to struggle free. 'Alright, alright, I done,' she said, suddenly releasing Rohini's head and moving to the sink to rinse the handkerchief, 'in one-two days the swelling go down. You know how I know?'

'How?' Rohini replied half-heartedly.

'How long you think I work for Massa Gladstone?' she asked and continued scrubbing the handkerchief without waiting for an answer. 'That's right. Since he was a boy growing up in this very house that belong to his uncle.' She squeezed out the handkerchief as if wringing a chicken's neck, as she did thrice a week for Gladstone's supper.

'Since he was a boy I know how to comfort my skin though it mark with weal and stripe.'

The morning after he had beaten her, Vidia woke up to the usual smell of curry and dhallpuri. She fed him as if nothing had happened, afterwards pouring clean water into a bucket for his bath. She laid out his clothes on the bed, the khaki half-trousers and string-vest he wore to work, which, after a day's labour in the canefield she washed dutifully. Today she awoke earlier than usual to put a fresh patch on his trousers. He watched her working her needle into the cloth, shocked at the sight of her bruised face. He was ashamed of his doing, but how else could he have responded when she confessed mixing poison into Kumar's dust and feeding it to the cow? He had to beat her. His mother Droopatie would have doused her in oil and scratched a match to her, so she should be thankful for his leniency. Should he have given her worse? As soon as she confessed, she had hurried to the kitchen, putting the puckni to her mouth and blowing into the fireside to awaken the cinders, as if challenging him to set her alight.

All morning he cut cane, wondering whether he had shown sufficient respect to his parents in merely beating her. When he returned home perhaps he should punish her with his cutlass. 'You think I shoulda wallop her more?' Vidia asked Kampta as they rested for lunch on the canal bank. Kampta, ten years or so older than Vidia, was a fellow cane cutter.

'Sure,' Kampta said, boredom evident in his voice. He guzzled down some bush-rum and passed the half-bottle to Vidia. Vidia hated drinking rum, especially during the day. It slowed down his work so that he made less money. He sipped some though, to bolster his image with Kampta. 'Give her your best,' Kampta said, 'chip her off at the root. After all, you is the most diligent coolie in the field.' He took the bottle from Vidia and swallowed a mouthful, gasping afterwards and spitting on the ground. 'Give me some tobacco, quick,' he gestured to Vidia, breaking into a cough.

'I don't smoke man.'

Kampta coughed some more then spat out a wad of phlegm into the canal. He rested on his elbows and watched it dissolve. A dragonfly hovered over it in uncertain flight, then darted off. When Kampta recovered his breath he poured the rest of the rum down his throat. Vidia watched him screw up his face and grind his teeth, wondering what made men allow themselves to be disfigured by rum. At least he, Vidia, had wife problems, but he still would not waste his money in liquor. He would cuff her about, as Kumar had once urged, then if nothing changed, he would do something else... but what he wasn't sure.

He needed a scamp like Kampta to advise him. Kampta cared for nothing and had told him so the first day they found themselves in the same work gang. During the rest period he pounced on Vidia, knowing him to be newly arrived and illiterate. He wore a leather pouch around his neck from which he extricated a piece of paper, unfolding it guardedly against the wind, as if it contained precious dust. 'This is my born-paper,' he told Vidia, 'which the whiteman sign. F-I-E-L-D-I-N-G. I spell it out for you because you stupid in English, no?'

Vidia nodded in shame yet eyed the lettering eagerly, wanting to learn.

'Here it say "Name", beside which whiteman write "Kampta". "Father's name: Unknown, deceased." "Mother's name: Unknown, deceased." "Grandmother's name: Unknown, deceased." "Date of Birth: Unknown." "Distinguishing marks: None." Everything is none or unknown or deceased, except my name in big-big writing, K-A-M-P-T-A.' He pointed the letters out to Vidia, dwelling on each one and when he reached the end he fell silent and lowered his face as if saddened by the brevity of the word. He recovered quickly though, and seeing Vidia still staring at the birth certificate he laughed cruelly at the boy, re-asserting his superiority. 'You know what your name look like in English?' he asked. 'Buy me two bottle rum and I show you.'

Vidia hesitated, wanting to offer something else instead of cash. 'You can count? I can show you how if you learn me to read.'

'Count? You stupid or what, boy? Why I should want to know to count? What there is for me to count?'

73

'How you mean? What about stars... stars and things like that...?'

Kampta broke out into more scornful laughter. 'You sure your head sound?' he asked. Vidia looked away. His abjectness made Kampta relent. 'Look. You here in Plantation Albion how long now? One-two year? Listen to me, because I born in this land and live here all my life. You gotta learn fast that you can only count what belong to you, and here you is nothing, nought, bruk-up calabash and rusty gill, you is 0. 0 plus 0 is 0. A coolie can multiply and minus quicker than whiteman can tally but a coolie is still 0. You know what 0 is? 0 is the shape of my nose-hole and mouth-hole and battie-hole, so a coolie does breathe and eat and shit day after day, year after year. Gladstone give me twenty-six cents a day so that all the 0's of my body can function till time come to die. How you will look up to the stars when Gladstone will keep your head forever bow to the root of cane?'

Kampta's outburst shocked Vidia. He was anxious not to be associated with such wild and dangerous opinions, and as the weeks passed he kept his distance, spending the lunch break instead with the boys who came over with him on the same boat. Kampta didn't miss him in the least. He continued to revel in his reputation for badness, taking delight in uttering Creole curses at the top of his voice or threatening to burn down Gladstone's house and the whole estate if his pay was not increased. He was a black-skinned coolie of suspected Madrasi ancestry, and he would behave accordingly. Gladstone expected nothing else of him. Only recently Gladstone had ordered that he be tied to a tree-trunk and whipped. He had stolen flour, rice, dried fish and brandy from Gladstone's store to take to a nigger bacchanal in a nearby village. Gladstone brought him before the district magistrate and declared him to be 'of an incorrigible and unrepentant nature'. Kampta was pleased that his behaviour had forced Gladstone into such proper English, whereas the villagers who gathered in the courtroom were terrified by the speech, wondering whether Kampta had not committed even greater crimes which Gladstone would disclose in due course. They had never before heard such words from his lips, accustomed only to his terse commands. 'Through birth and rearing in the colony he has taken on nigger values to add to his Madrasi instincts for trouble-someness; he is indolent, thievish and cunning, and seeks the company of lewd and faithless Creole women in preference to the sobriety of a settled relationship. He has no sense of the rights of ownership and in stealing from his fellow coolies – a crime to which he is habituated – he creates a web of accusation and counter-accusation among them, which is detrimental to the welfare of the Plantation. The loss of his property causes acute distress to a coolie. It will provoke the most docile of them to the kind of barbarism that breaks out in India randomly and for no apparent reason other than the conditioning of centuries which no English effort can reverse.'

And with that, Kampta was given three months' work without wages and fourteen strokes each Sunday afternoon for the duration of the sentence.

The punishment took place in Gladstone's garden, underneath the star-apple tree, and coolies newly landed in the Plantation were summoned to witness it. The first few Sundays were solemn affairs, the obvious pain that Kampta suffered acting as a successful deterrent. They left the compound morosely, and the next day they chopped away at the cane as if their lives depended on it. It was the niggers who relaxed them, turning out in increasing numbers to witness the beating and bringing mischief to the scene. 'Coolies! welcome to the colony!' one called out between whiplashes, 'all-you come to steal we work and wages but scab will form instead on your arse.' 'Chastise the heathen, cleanse him of iniquities,' another sang to a Christian tune, satirising his own progress yet delighting in the sonorousness of the words. Others took the opportunity of doing hard business. A nigger seller wandered into the yard with cages of parrots but the coolies would not buy so he spat in their direction and departed. Fellow pedlars touted cow-skin purses, cotton vests, and bottles of herbal medicines. When Miriam appeared, the crowd fell silent. She wore a cotton dress of gaudy colours, tight-fitting around her buttocks but slit along the front to reveal torn stockings. She called out in a brazen voice. The coolies ceased milling around the star-apple tree and stared at her aimlessly.

The remaining Sundays became occasions of festivity, the coolies squatting in the grass and unwrapping rotis and potato curry whilst their children ran about with home-made kites. A nigger fiddler, glad for a taste of free food and rum, joined the picnic, slapping the frail backs of a few coolies in a show of instant camaraderie. The food jolted free from their hands or mouths. Pieces of potato lay on the grass and the nigger fiddler smiled maliciously as ants scrambled over them. Miriam came and sat in their midst. She spread her legs wide and when she closed them a faint puff of talcum powder escaped through the slit in her dress. A few coolies slinked off to a safe distance, unable to finish their food. Others proffered handfuls of channa, fascinated by the way her bosom swung with her neck each time she turned to curse Kampta. 'He owe me five dollar, but still I keep giving him credit,' she explained, 'why God make me so big-hearted?' And she pushed out her chest at them as if to prove the point. She chewed some palouri then spat it out, scraping the remains on her tongue with her forefinger. 'Pepper! pepper!' she screamed, grabbing a cup of coconut water from the hand of a coolie whilst pushing him violently to one side.

When the beating ended the ropes were loosened and Kampta sagged to the foot of the star-apple tree, hugging the trunk to save him slipping into unconsciousness. The bark bruised his arms, arousing fresh, sharp pain which he concentrated upon so as to forget the greater pain slicing with slow, rusty movements into his back. A breeze played mercifully under the edges of his skin where it was torn. Gladstone left the balcony where he had witnessed the beating and entered his house. The coolies, alert to Gladstone's every gesture, even though seemingly absorbed in the fun, gathered up their belongings and departed immediately. None dared to jeopardise their welfare by offering to help Kampta, and as they filed towards the gate he raised his head with his last strength and grinned at them. A nigger gang came up immediately, cut him loose, laid him in a makeshift stretcher and took him to their village. Miriam led the procession like one carrying home the spoils of some tribal war. Whenever they passed a coolie hut she drew in her breath and expanded her chest to make her body appear even bigger and more intimidating. 'So whiteman bleed the badness out of your arse,' she mocked Kampta in a voice loud enough to carry to their ears. 'Coolie like you can never compare to nigger people. All-you got talk but all-you only cowardly.' She sucked her teeth at a group of coolie villagers gathered in the forecourt of the rumshop. 'You call yourselves man,' she shouted at one of them as he raised a bottle to his mouth, 'but the only man in this colony is Mr Gladstone. The rest of you only sporting cock between your leg by accident. God mean to give you a slit but he make mistake.'

'Gwan, you black-rass bitch,' one man threatened her, 'casreep bubbling from your scunt and congregating flies. Go wash yourself of stinkiness.' Miriam advanced towards the forecourt as if to cuff out his teeth but the coolie stood his ground. 'Come one more step let me hold you down and jaray you,' he cackled, undoing the string holding up his trousers, 'I hear black pussy taste like when you suck on a piece of raw liver, not so Kampta? Kampta, is true nigger pokey-hair hard like wire broom and scratch up your face when you go down to suck? I hear you got to close your eyes when you go down in case the hairs juk them out and blind you, not so?'

She turned away, flouncing about her buttocks disdainfully. 'Talk. Only talk all-you have. Once Gladstone raise his hand that carrying the whip, all-you shut up quick-quick. Look at that one!' She pointed at Kampta who lay passively in the stretcher, barely able to raise a groan. 'That is coolie condition, God be witness to the truth. Flat on your coolie back with your two-inch cock impossible to raise howsoever I gallivant before it.' She clicked her fingers and the nigger stretcher-bearers continued their journey, pausing whenever they passed a coolie hut to allow her to heap more insults upon Kampta.

'Easy man, easy,' she chided them when they reached her yard and no coolies were in sight.

'Is only a coolie dog, you yourself say so,' one muttered as they tilted Kampta rudely out of the stretcher. He fell heavily on the ground and rolled over on his back. Dust and grit entered the open wounds. He screamed in sudden pain, kicking out madly at the niggers and trying to raise his body to assault them, 'Eh! eh! look at that ungrateful crab-dog coolie,' one cursed, picking up a stick and waving it over Kampta, waiting for him to struggle upright so as to beat him down again. Miriam strode over and in one swoop hauled it out of his hand. 'Who you calling coolie, you ugly black monkey-face Madrasi?'

'Me no Madrasi, me is nigger, so watch your mouth,' he retaliated, trying to snatch the stick back from her.

'Me no Madrasi, me is nigger… me no Madrasi…' she jeered in a high-pitched voice as if imitating a parrot. She pushed her head forwards as if to peck him and ran her hand along the stick, assessing its bluntness. 'Out-out,' she shouted after him, slapping the stick wilfully against her side as if whipping a mule, 'haul your stinkness from my yard before I coolie your backside. Next time you call my man coolie is the last time you preserve teeth and tongue in your mouth, you hear? What is you but always a nigger?'

She stood squarely at the gate and stared after them as they retreated, perplexed by the way she had suddenly turned against them. When they were safely out of sight she went back to Kampta, kneeling at his back and trying to blow loose dirt from the raw edges of his wounds. 'Three hundred years of sin can't just wash away like that even if they bathe in Jordan river till Jesus come again! Nigger is nigger is nigger.' She called out fiercely to her brothers who came running out of the hut with pieces of rags and a bucket of boiling water. 'Why you hide whilst nigger man raise stick against me?' she accused them. 'You have no shame or what? Whiteman beat strongness out of you, make you turn your face whilst your sister rape? Kampta surely right to scorn you. He lying bruk-up at your foot but he is a stubborn man, a special nigger.' They handed her the rags, rested the bucket beside her, not daring to meet her eyes. They looked sheepishly at Kampta instead as if to discover the dignity that had eluded them. Kampta only groaned as Miriam dabbed the water on his skin. 'A special nigger,' Miriam asserted in spite of Kampta's obvious wretchedness, 'in no time he would rise up and bring calamity to Albion and burn down the canefields and turn Gladstone into a pillar of salt.' They shifted uncomfortably around Kampta's body, wanting to snigger, at the same time assuming a respectful aspect whenever Miriam looked up. She was crazy in truth and beyond control, but since their father had died when they were still young – one barely able to walk seven steps without tumbling on to his face, the older two helplessly malnourished – and their mother had picked up without warning and run away to another village, it was Miriam, twelve years old, who had succoured them. She had found work in the Great House, looking after Gladstone who was five years or so older than her. She washed and pressed his clothes, cleaned his room, put away his books. He took her hunting, giving her charge of the birds retrieved by his dogs – she wrung the necks of the wounded before bundling them up with the dead. For twenty years she had tended to him, indoors and outdoors, learning to pacify him, and the snarling dogs which would savage her hand at the first careless or inconfident move. She had provided for her brothers until they could walk to fetch water or grow arms strong enough to handle cutlass and shovel; crazy as she was they would never dare to contradict her.

'Get out of the light,' she commanded, waving them away, 'you throwing such a shadow over the man I can't see red from black.' When they were out of earshot she resumed bathing Kampta's wounds, taunting him at the same time for surrendering to Gladstone. 'Why you drop on your knee and quake after they done with you, and make Gladstone smirk? Why you didn't spit at him after each lash? But no, you stiffen, then you sag, like if they make you come, eh? Like if Gladstone fasten on your cock and drain you, eh? How you think *I* feel when I see you yield to that bugger-battie man, you think anything about *me*, you dog you?' And she rubbed the rag spitefully along the groove of a wound, making him cry out even in his comatose state. The noise made her relent: at least he was being attentive to her. 'Dog, you still owe me five dollar,' she addressed him tenderly, 'don't think is love I doing this for.' She patted his back dry and then began teasing the edges of loose skin with the gentlest of touches, straightening them where they had curled upwards and stiffened in dried blood. 'Still, you can accumulate debt with me, I ain't no coolie with coin. How come all-you coolie people stay so? How come all-you people worship coin with whiteman face on it?' She ripped the rags into strips as if to express her contempt, then began to bandage him. 'No, I give you one-hundred dollar credit for pussy, but one cent after that and you got to marry me. Marry me, you hear? You can't pay back, howsoever much you bribe me with interest. You is the only interest I want, you hear, you coolie dog!' And when he groaned she sat back on her heels and rocked her salted body with laughter.

Miriam knew Kampta for as many years as she served Gladstone. And she fancied that his hatred of Gladstone went beyond the normal resentment that the coolies felt because of Gladstone's power over them. It was her doings in the Great House which goaded Kampta; that he could not witness or interfere with them, since he could not enter the House, maddened him further. She belonged to Gladstone, together with his punts, his fields, his work gangs, his mules, his books, his pictures and the collection of furniture, china and cutlery she knew intimately, having grown up in the midst of such finery, having cleaned and polished them as if they were her own. 'When he dead Gladstone will leave everything for me,' she joked but he was in no mood for humour.

'*Everything* is *me*, not that insect. I don't care what he own, he is only insect and will born so in next life.'

'Hush your mouth with all that heathen talk, you want get me dismiss from service or what?' she reproached him playfully.

'Sandfly, hookworm or malabunta, nothing less. Coolie people from India stupid in everything but they right about what form you take when you born again. Gladstone will come back as a beetle moving in cow dung and latrine slime.' He stooped, picked up a stone and pelted it with all his strength into the bush beyond her yard. It clipped the edge of a huge skaps' nest clinging cancerously to the trunk of a jamoon tree. He threw another stone, this time into the heart of the nest, relishing the chaos as it ruptured.

It was not always like this, his raging, his foolish ambition to overcome Gladstone even in his empty-handed state. True, he had turned up in the same beaten condition as now, but as a boy stumbling into her yard, barely able to raise his hand to beg a drink of water. He had walked three or four days through bush, avoiding the main paths in case he was re-captured and returned to Plantation Fielding. His parents had fallen to malaria in the middle of their indentureship, leaving no savings behind. He was only a child at the time, but the plantation owner still laid claim to his labour in lieu of the loss of his parents and the money he had laid out to secure their passage from India. Kampta offered dismal tales of constant beating from the coolies who had taken him in but who resented the need to feed an unproductive child.

'Why they adopt you when all the time they reckoning the money they squander to feed you?' she asked, doubting him.

'Because we is Indian people and we stay so. Everybody is family to everybody.'

'But why they abuse you then and make you eat what fowl and swine leave behind?'

'Because I don't grow up quick enough for canefield work and slave for them in their old age.'

She listened, caught between compassion and disbelief. It was always like this with him – he could work up the most distressing story, manipulating her into dishing out whatever meagre food was in the pot. He ate savagely, knowing that she and her brothers would go without until she acquired the next day's rations. As she watched the contentment on his face she wanted to snatch the plate and chase him from her yard. Still, she let him eat, and he stayed on to take advantage of the gifts Gladstone bestowed upon her in return for her service.

She passed him off to the coolies as a cousin from another village – his dark skin, darker than hers, and tightly curled hair made it easy for him to be taken for a half-caste. The coolies feared him immediately, his negroid appearance presaging what awaited their daughters in the future, if they lingered too long in the colony. They ignored him altogether, as if he didn't exist, and the silence they kept made it possible to keep his history a secret from Gladstone who would have sent him back to Plantation Fielding. He fitted into the household with perfect ease, striking up an instant friendship with her brothers. They were slow-witted and clumsy in expression whereas he could conjure up stories at will to entertain and ensnare them. 'Tell we jumbie story,' the brothers would beg, and without hesitating he would invent murderers for them, each named after himself. 'Who you want Kampta kill

– preacherman or beggarman, foreman or poorman?' he asked, enumerating the victims on his fingers as if the brothers were idiots. 'All ten,' Peter shouted, being the youngest, but Kampta ignored him and told of Kampta, the cane cutter, who secured his wife's limbs with cow-wire, tied cloth around her mouth, stripped her and placed her outside in a nest of centipedes to be stung all night whilst he retired to bed to sleep. She bit into the cloth, trying to loosen it, to let out a scream, but a centipede slid under it into her mouth, stung her throat and nestled in the hot swelling flesh to lay its young. The next morning, Kampta the cane cutter pierced the cloth, opened his wife's mouth and fished out the contented centipede on the tip of his cutlass. The more it wriggled the more it became impaled, until, utterly exhausted, its belly slid along the blade in a slow suicide.

'Man, how come you so small and talk such total nastiness?' Miriam asked him. 'Where you learn about chopping and making baby and everything?'

'Rumshop,' he said, surprised at the naïvety of her question.

'How you mean rumshop?'

'Rumshop, you know, rumshop. Where big man does sit and drunk up and talk what he do with woman in India, and Law allow it because things stay so in India. Since I small I hang around Fielding rumshop and listen how all them big man does roar and make murderation...' He fell silent as if recovering the details of what he had witnessed. 'I frighten you? Tell the truth, the jumbie stories I tell frighten you?' he blurted out, seeking her approval.

'Gwan!' She sucked her teeth and laughed. 'Nothing frighten me. You think I don't know blood and thing?'

'Thomas and Joe and Peter frighten like hell! I frighten them so bad they make space for me!'

'Them is small boys, they wet their pants when darkness come and I don't appear,' she said dismissively. 'No, you don't frighten me. One cuff from me and your mouth keep silence for all time!' She stared at him, taking pleasure when he retreated into himself. He clenched his jaw and gazed at his feet, at a patch of dust, focusing with such energy that he became oblivious of her presence. It was a trick he must have learnt and practised to make bearable all the beatings he claimed to have suffered.

'Tell me nice story, you know any nice story?' she asked, softening towards him. It was the end of a day in which Gladstone had behaved in his peculiar manner with her. No marks were visible on her skin, it was more a weariness within. It was an intimate feeling for she had become habituated to working for Gladstone. The familiarity of it consoled her. She knew that she would get up in the morning and start freshly again, making enough to feed all of them, with the odd luxuries that Gladstone supplied in penitence – English salmon in a tin painted brightly with a picture of English gentlewomen picnicking in a meadow, or a jar of cocoa with a label of beautiful English lettering – making her life special compared to the rest of the plantation.

'Tell me nice story, nuh,' she insisted. They were propped against the outside wall doing nothing but waiting for sleep. Kampta dug his heels in the dust of the yard, making aimless holes. He fidgeted whenever the moon exposed his face. He fixed his eyes on the thick, almost fleshy darkness surrounding the hut. He felt safe within the livery of the night.

'How you mean nice story?'

'Nice, you know, just nice.'

'I only tell jumbie story,' he said tensely, rubbing some dirt from his forehead and rolling it into a ball. He squashed it between thumb and forefinger into a small black puri, rounded it again into a palouri, then let it fall. He dug more dirt from his skin, making new shapes of food. She sensed his agitation and decided to let the conversation rest for his sake, but it was he who re-started it.

'You hear the jumbie story I tell Thomas and them about Kampta cacka-hole?' he asked.

'Man I don't want to hear any more misery from your mouth,' she threatened, refusing to let him bully her as he did her brothers. They were terrified of him, doing the weeding and planting of the garden whilst he lazed like an overseer under the shade of a coconut tree. He would get up occasionally to stick some ochro seeds into the earth they had prepared, as if to justify his boarding and lodging with them, then go back to relaxing under the tree, staring for ever into its branches, concocting fresh stories to subdue them.

'And all your coolie words don't cow me neither, chala, haal, backna, and all that paganness. If you want remain in my yard then you better start behave nice,' Miriam threatened.

'You mean nice like how Gladstone does treat you?' he retaliated, then, startled at his own boldness, drew his knees up to lessen his body. She looked confusedly at him, caught between the hurt of his question and scorn for his cowardice.

'What you know about Mr Gladstone and me?' She felt exhausted again; not the tiredness that gladly sought sleep but one that gnawed at her, keeping her in a vague state of rage and apathy.

'When you say "nice", is story you want hear about kiskidee building nest, and frangipani, and how hibiscus smell sweet as it look?' he asked to distract her from his rudeness. He regretted his descent into gentleness and added immediately, 'you mean story like girl them does talk?' She didn't answer, withdrawing into herself, surrendering to the pity of her situation. 'If only Ma come back soon,' she said, wanting to cry but her eyes remained stubbornly clear. It was so when she was with Gladstone – whatever the grief, no tears would come, and he took her resilience as a sign of emotional coarseness, the condition of a mule which would endure dozens of lashes before it brayed. When she thought of it she could never remember crying, not even as a child.

'You did cry plenty when your people beat you?' she asked. Perhaps she was no ordinary nigger, perhaps the fact she couldn't cry meant God had marked her out for some special happening, as the preacherman said he did to Mary who made a baby without man's interference.

'Why your Ma run away?' he replied, ignoring her question.

'Because she turn mad, why else you think?'

'Don't get vex, I only asking. At least my Ma dead out on me and not desert.'

'Well my mother desert we – which take more strength than your mother had,' she said proudly, 'after fifteen years borning and raising we, she wake up early-morning and decide to vanish. But first she pick up a stick and come to the bed where Thomas and Joe and Peter and me sleeping and she let loose some lash. You should hear screaming but she never stop till the stick bruk in two over my shoulder. She stand for a minute to catch her breath, then she turn and stamp out of the hut…'

'Your mother mad for true! What you do make her become so?' Kampta wondered, looking at her with new admiration.

'*My* shoulder. Why *my* shoulder? What wrong with Thomas shoulder? He big enough also to take blow. Joe and Peter still small but Thomas nearly tall like me, so why she select me when I work from since I can walk, scrubbing clothes, cleaning trench, cooking for everybody, till one day Gladstone spot me on the backdam bend like a piece of wire under a sackful of copra which I take to sell in market, and he look kindly on me, climb down the pony he riding to give me a dollar for the sack which he throw in the bush, and next morning I start labour for him till today, two years soon. So why me? Why me? When Ma gone I sit in a corner and open my mouth to cry. Even now I open my mouth and cry still don't come, and she don't come…'

'I can make you cry,' he offered, feeling foolish as soon as he uttered the words. He moved towards her, wanting to comfort her but not knowing how to touch her.

'If Massa Gladstone can't, what cause a backward coolie boy like you think you will overcome me?' she asked, suddenly rearing up and breaking into forced laughter as he withdrew in shame.

'Niggerman digging in your belly for gold that belong to me,' Vidia screamed, hitting Rohini in the face. She buried her head in her arms to shield it from his attack.

'What niggerman? What niggerman?' she cried, not so much in terror of the blows but of what he had become. Only two years previously, in India, he would not have conceived of hurting her. It was she who taunted him for being timid, daring him to leave his parents, daring him to threaten to stone Kumar's head until Kumar told him where the rupees were buried. She stunned him by the cruelty of her plans. She made him serve her by stealing food from Droopatie's kitchen and taking it secretly to her mother. She demanded he picked firewood for Finee or help dig her garden. As he laboured in her yard, Finee reproached herself for once standing in the way of Rohini's marriage. The boy was meek and diligent, the very picture of Jagnat. Finee wanted to call him in to nourish him, if only her breasts had not become husks, if only Rohini was not always watching suspiciously from Droopatie's verandah, waiting for him to return.

'What Ma make you do?' Rohini demanded when he came home, noticing his face running with sweat.

'Nothing,' he said, wiping himself on the towel she gave him. When he handed it back she examined the smear of wet dirt, working herself up into a passion.

'How do you mean "nothing"?' she hissed, turning her back to him, lifting her blouse to her neck, and dabbing her breast with the towel. She confronted him again, pulling her blouse down before he could catch more than a glimpse of her breasts.

Droopatie was visiting her daughter in the next village, and Vidia's father was snoring contentedly in the hammock outside, having been lotioned by her hands. She watched his leg flopping indiscreetly over the side of the hammock. She had Vidia to herself – a rare moment which she would savour like the papaya he fetched her before she bit into its seeds for a taste of bitterness.

'"Nothing" make you sweat so?' she asked, flinging the towel to the ground. 'Droopatie gone, so all day *I* sweat in kitchen and *I* sweat in bedroom and before *I* can catch my breath your Pa come home. But no, "nothing" make you sweat, eh? Tell me, two hours you stay at Ma house doing "nothing" and still sweating?'

'But I been weeding the yard for her as you tell me,' he said, hesitating to protest louder in the hope that she would raise her blouse again.

She was as bewildered by her mood as he was, but she could not rest from challenging him. 'Weeding? How come you spend two hours weeding and Ma garden only the size of your… the size of your cock?' Her outburst so took him by surprise that he stooped automatically to pick up the towel. She watched him wringing it into a rope, suspecting that she had gone too far. She changed tactics, lowered her voice and rebuked him for not coming to her earlier.

'You know I stay here all day, your Ma gone till night, and still you delay. Why you not leave the goats and Ma yard and hurry back, how I pine for you. But no, Ma waylay you, and you linger with her.'

'But *you* tell me to weed the yard and from the verandah you see me,' he repeated, the towel taut in his hand.

'If I tell you to put your mouth here what you will do?' she asked, pulling him towards her breasts. As he snuggled there she looked out of the hut to the dishevelled figure of his father. She regretted her weakness. Why was she afraid of Vidia? Husband or not, if he only raised his hand she would scream loudly enough to awaken his father. She knew she could depend on his father. If she commanded, he would dash Vidia to the ground, he would wrench the boy up by the neck and choke him to within a breath of his life. Only a further scream from Rohini would induce him to release Vidia. She looked down at him burrowing into her waist, resolving to scream and summon his father if he moved an inch lower.

'What niggerman?' Rohini cried, falling to Vidia's feet and clutching them in case he kicked her in the stomach. But his rage was spent as suddenly as it had arisen; he stood over her in a daze, alarmed at his capacity to hurt her. Was it so easy to raise his feet and stun her with a kick, and when she buckled and fell, mash her head into the ground with his heel as if mashing out the life of a centipede? He looked around the room, noticing for the first time how all the humble implements they used to keep their marriage together – bellna, puckni, tawa, cutlass – could so easily become the means of a dozen brutal ways of harming her. He pushed her away and went outside, avoiding the coolies lounging around camp-fires getting drunk. Their only consolation was rum, but the more they drank, the more they grieved inwardly for wives abandoned in India. He knew that the longer he left Rohini the more danger he faced from them. Only yesterday Kampta had related what happened to a woman in a neighbouring estate. The woman's husband was sick. He had been wretched for weeks, and the lonely coolies were waiting for his death so they could claim his wife. He lingered on beyond their patience; fortified by rum they broke down the door, chopped him to a mess, then dragged his wife to a respectable distance. 'But beside which, it coulda been *her* encouragement that make them behave so, you believe?' Kampta asked, looking cunningly at him, 'woman them does beg for vile botheration.' Vidia pretended not to hear, slashing noisily at the cane. He didn't want to compare Rohini's behaviour to the raped woman's, though it was true that since coming to Guiana their love-making had become more peculiar. Rohini lay brazenly on the floor and demanded of him. She rolled over shamelessly and he pierced her from behind. Sometimes she gave him pain, clawing his flesh yet stopping his mouth with her hand to prevent the pain escaping. He would struggle to throw her off but, with cunning anticipation, she would release her grip, letting the pain subside. Her timing and her manoeuvres so fulfilled him that afterwards he no longer cared whether or not she would make a baby. The separation from India and from his parents seemed a separation from a shameful immaturity. Now he was a man, even though his wife was slow in bearing. Still, his money would grow, and his status with the other coolies. He could wait for a house of children, as Rohini taught him to wait inside her body; not rupturing in a boyish flow but waiting for the perfect moment, like a papaya turning from green to yellow to ochre before she commanded him to pick it.

'Vile botheration.' Kampta's words provoked Vidia long after he was out of earshot of the drunken coolies. He hurried to the calabash tree, but felt no real desire to dig up his jars. He squatted under the branches, sharing the space with its nigger spirits with whom he was now familiar. How often had he come to this spot to follow the rhythm of their voices? Voices that started up manfully, but quickly dipped; voices that struggled to break out from the burial places, from the roots of kaita or pik trees choking their mouths. A maku squawked in sudden pain as a rat seized it and the bush became alive with the noises of dread; palima birds calling to each other for reassurance, juka monkeys quickly gathering their young and howling defiance. The rat feasted and was content. It slipped back into its hole to rest, to wait for another night. The danger passed, the noise died, and Vidia listened once more to the voices of the dead, nigger victims fluting through slit throats. No, he was not afraid of them, as his fellow coolies were. They would not harm him, because he came from a land that bore no malice to niggers. Before coming to Guiana he had never known that there were people like niggers. In Plantation Albion he bore no responsibility for the mound of earth in the deep backdam that marked their mass burial. The other coolies had somehow learned of its existence and they whispered fearfully among themselves, warning newcomers like himself to avoid it. No one was sure where the mound was. No one had actually seen it, but stories abounded that somewhere beyond the clearing of canefields, where the land was pure jungle, the nigger spirits lived. The bodies of some fifty men and women slain by old Gladstone were dumped there. No one knew why old Gladstone had them killed. They were healthy and productive. They hatched no plot to rebel. Why would old Gladstone squander his wealth so freely? The bones gathered dirt and the debris of the jungle, over time growing into a sterile mound. Not even the hardiest weed could take root on it. And the jungle animals avoided burrowing into its side, or building their nests on it.

The nigger spirits slept in the hollows of trees, dreaming of their villages in Africa, but it was an unwholesome sleep. They awoke in moments of rage to curse the cane, to curse old Gladstone and his descendants, to curse the waters which bore no memory of their passage, no memory or trail to guide them back to Africa. It was then that clouds broke over Demerara, washing away topsoil and drowning the young shoots, or the Atlantic spilled over the land, choking the canals with sand and salt. But it was a useless rage, causing only slight damage to the Plantation, and the nigger spirits gave up and went back to sleep.

The rhythm of rage and sleep... Vidia had heard it at nights, in the solitude of bush, when he alone was awake, sharing the earth with the dead. He had seen the same rhythm in the daytime among the living nigger work gangs. They resented their tasks, idling whenever the overseer was distracted, stealing whatever Plantation tools they could lay their hands on to exchange, not for money, but for cloth. They held no pride in their work, only in their appearance. When it came to dressing up for a fête, the shabbiest nigger cane cutter transformed himself instantly into a dandy, teeth scrubbed and polished, skin perfumed. All was appearance with them, which was why he didn't bother when they threatened to strike or to smash up the sugar factory. He knew their rage would spend itself as unpredictably as it arose, or give way to the smallest bribe from Gladstone – a few pieces of cloth with which to make party costumes, and strips of leather to furnish their feet. They blamed the slave past for their present shabbiness, but what was their past? He had overheard the older coolies speaking in appalled tones about Africa, a place of disease, worse than India. The niggers lived there in horribly unmanageable numbers. Food was short so they ate each other but still their numbers grew. Diseases arose vengefully from the soil – the bacteria of previous murdered generations – to wipe out whole communities almost, but the outpouring of wombs soon filled the patches, or else niggers appeared mysteriously from elsewhere to settle. Babies or beggars or bodies sleek with malnutrition whilst priests fattened on their superstitions... Africa would go on for ever, an endless supply of victims. The whiteman shipped countless of them to Guiana to teach them how to read and write, how to work, but they were beyond disinfection; neither Bible nor beatings could break their habits.

Is that why he constantly felt like hitting Rohini? Was she learning from the niggers how to do it in shameless ways, spreading her legs and opening her mouth? He could never figure out how she knew to do it. The first time it happened, under the tamarind tree in India, she pushed him off, brushed the dust from her legs and walked away wordlessly. It was as if she had done it so often that it was only a routine for her, a household task. Later he confided in Kumar but Kumar only increased his confusion by talk of blood. What blood? How was he to know that the first time girls did it they bled? It was dark anyway under the tamarind tree – how was he to distinguish sweat from blood? Kumar laughed and laughed. Vidia stared into his mouth, seeing the laughter slithering off his tongue as he had slithered off Rohini's body when she had finished with him.

'Vile botheration,' Kampta told him, 'and Guiana itself breed vileness in woman. Pig breeding pig, mule mounting mule, scorpions building nest, and ants, and snakes laying eggs, and everything fucking in the open and fertile. No wonder bush take over coolie woman. And no matter how furious you hack, you still can't clear enough space. Bush and vine suck her in for all time. Best take her back to India. At least all you got there is dust and drought and manfolk studying their bellies how they so hungry, they don't care their cocks drop off because the whole place sterile anyway. But then again how come coolie people breed so much in India even though they hardly got strength to take down their panty? How come, eh?'

Vidia didn't know. He squatted under the calabash tree in the midst of the nigger spirits who sobbed and grieved not knowing why the whiteman had murdered them. The desire to dig up his jars and count his money returned. Only money made sense. It didn't proliferate like womb and bush, but grew steadily, one coin added cautiously to the next, the sum total always true. You could count and re-count and always arrive at the same number. Money was safe, it was faithful. He was glad that he wasn't as wealthy as Gladstone who owned so much that he couldn't keep control of his possessions, couldn't keep an accurate inventory of them. Gladstone couldn't even trust the value of his estate for it fluctuated according to the weather which could devastate the crop. Tiny worms and invisible germs could cause blight, could bring down his mighty estate. Gladstone could so easily go crazy just thinking about how much he owned yet couldn't count, couldn't rely on. No wonder, now and again, he ordered a coolie to be tied to a tree and whipped. One tree, one coolie, one whip: it was simple arithmetic. He, Vidia, would be content for the moment with his few jars. He would add evenly to the jars and when they held sufficient coins he would empty the lot and buy a small plot to build on. Then he would start saving slowly and deliberately again, always keeping the numbers small and simple. It would prevent him going crazy like Gladstone, and wanting to beat Rohini. From now on he would dedicate himself to saving and counting his money, and to no other pleasure. Next time Rohini wanted sex he would do it with control. She heaved and squealed and stabbed at his flesh, wanting, always wanting – like Gladstone galloping the length of his plantation, rearing his whip at a startled coolie for no reason except madness had seized his brain; madness because no matter how resolutely he gripped the rein he still panicked about the proportions of his wealth. He, Vidia, would content himself with a small, known amount of money. And when Rohini bore a boy-child he would stop the madness and pain and greed of sleeping with her.

The Gladstone family cemetery, a plot laid with lawn and adorned with urns of hibiscus and frangipani, was Miriam's favourite retreat. It was within the compound of the Great House, surrounded by a high wall of Suffolk brick especially shipped over from England. Neither nigger nor goat could idle in to graze, for the entrance was barred by an iron gate. Of all the workers in the Plantation, including the gardeners who tended the plot, only she had the key – a special favour from Gladstone. To wander among the white dead, to unwrap her bundle of fruit and picnic in their presence, and when the sun was sluggishly hot, to lean up against them: this was her special privilege. The white gravestones glared at her. She closed her eyes and held her breath, pretending to be the last corpse. The effort of suppressing her breath made sweat rush to the surface of her skin. She let out the air in a loud wheeze and cackled to herself at the thought of her livingness. Fuck-ass dead white babies... no black hands to wipe their backsides now, no black lips to tune up a lullaby! She grabbed a broad leaf from off a sadu tree and fanned her body indelicately. God was watching her through the vast, cloudless sky. God's iris *was* the sky, blue like whiteman's, but she didn't care what He saw. Fifty thousand million white angel-stars stopped twinkling, shocked at what she and Kampta did, but blood-cloth to the lot of them! When she died they could blow upon her and disperse her in particles of dust throughout the universe so that she could never again be gathered up. Well let that time come, amen. For the moment she was here, and fat, and Kampta was sprightly upon her, so that when they arose, no imprint was left on the earth, no definite shape which was hers. No matter how he grunted and pressed, he was still too slight a coolie to leave a trace of her in the earth.

'I ain't going to bury in some nigger mound in backdam,' she told Rohini, giving her a tour of the cemetery as a way of impressing her status upon the lesser servant. 'You see that one over there, my one will be big and shiny so.' She led Rohini to what was the most ornamental grave in the plot. The headstone was carved with cherubim holding up laurels or blowing trumpets. At the corners of the tomb were urns bearing a profusion of bright, tropical flowers which reflected colours on to the stone, giving it a gaiety absent from the rest of the graves. An ornamental pond patterned with lilies lay before it, softening the appearance of the stone. They stood at the foot of the pond looking at the tomb's reflection; fish seeped through it as if through stone, scaling the interior with tropical colour. The gloomy dead English body of old Mrs Gladstone lay there, but swimming within it were bright cubla and maju fish… the bitch didn't deserve more than dry, white dust but all good things come to whitepeople even in death. Jelly fish and piranha would have filled the pond if Miriam had her way.

'Who bury here?' Rohini asked in a whisper, awed by the beauty of the setting.

'Old Mrs Gladstone. It say on the headset. You can't read Latin?'

'Little bit.' Rohini stared at the lettering.

'The top is the Latin, and the bottom write in English.'

'Acha,' Rohini nodded in agreement.

'Sunt Lachrimae Rerum. You can understand that?'

'I only learning… the English more easy than what write on top.'

'Sunt Lachrimae Rerum… to tell the truth, girl, I ignorant myself what it betoken.'

'But how you know to talk the words?' Rohini asked, overwhelmed by Miriam's learning.

'My grandpa tell me how. No nigger in this plantation blacker than he, but Latin he know, what old whitepeople used to write in book. He was stonemason, and everytime whiteman die, is my grandpa who they instruct to carve plaque and letter it with Latin they write down for him on piece paper. All over this place, Gladstone graveyard, Anglican church, Plantation House, my grandpa work so hard that he learn Latin. He speak nigger-talk and he speak Latin and he used to say that two of them cousin-close like bastards from one belly. Sunt is like scunt. Lachrimae sound like old Mrs Gladstone's name and Rerum is rear up, what preacherman does call resurrection. So the old scunt Lachrimae will break wind and break stone and walk the land when Kingdom come, and nigger once more will scatter at her footstep.'

'How she dead?' Rohini asked, seeking a direct response from Miriam, something simpler than the story of her grandpa's doings.

'Childbirth. She was bearing but like the child violent and kick up her stomach and kill her.' Miriam looked hard at Rohini, sensing the girl's withdrawal from her. She felt a sudden compassion for Rohini, for someone who still believed in giving birth, as she once did. Someone to love was what she wanted but she got Gladstone and Kampta instead. All of them – the whole Plantation of niggers and coolies – saw only her fat and her rudeness. She, Miriam, was good to get drunk with, to curse and grope and guffaw; they wanted her to slap them away in mock anger. They admired her strength when she pushed them off and they fell on the rumshop floor, a humiliation more acceptable than that they suffered at Gladstone's hand. She knew her status among them, as someone who could roam among the master's possessions and throughout his estate with the freedom they lacked. They provoked her to outrageous deeds, for every show of rudeness was a sign of their own desire. To begin with she accepted her status dutifully, for the sake of restoring their pride. She was looking after her three abandoned brothers and she would take in the rest of the tribe. She would nurture them all until they grew strong enough to survive on their own.

She remembered her grandpa coming home with a bruised mouth because a big word he had acquired from some gravestone had slipped out in the presence of a whiteman who took his learning as a sign of arrogance. For weeks after, her grandpa would talk like a nigger, using a dozen small words at the most, and mispronouncing them ignorantly. Only when his mouth was healed and the pain diminished would he try out the odd phrase, but even so muttering to himself. Each morning she went into the adjoining yard, where he lived, with a bowl of boiled plantains for his breakfast. He was once inside his hut sharpening his chisel for the day's work when the file slipped and injured his thumb. He screamed some Latin involuntarily. When she rushed in, he raised his hand protectively to his mouth and babbled apologies, as if expecting a whiteman. The shame on his face afterwards was a nigger shame; it was inscribed on all their faces. She had always seen it, even when they twisted their looks to feign anger or revengefulness. The louder they slapped their hands down on the rumshop table the more clearly the scars of their humiliation showed. But the burden of sustaining their pride was outweighed by shame for their cowardice. Only Kampta was deserving of her. For all the beatings from Gladstone he came and went as he pleased. He would abscond from the plantation on a whim and disappear into the bush. They were all terrified of the bush. The whiteman had made them clear the land, creating paths, digging canals. He gave them a space within the estate which they became habituated to. Each morning they left their logies and walked down certain dams to their assigned portions of canefields. Each evening they returned home along familiar paths. New generations arose but they too moved in the same direction, for the same purpose. They felt secure within the design of Gladstone's estate. The boldest dared to trespass in the forbidden spaces *within* the estate, received their lashes when caught, and retreated back to their logies. Not even the boldest dared to test its boundaries, though, by entering the bush at the back of the estate. Except Kampta. He cast off his clothes and joined up with the Amerindian tribes, living savagely on their diet of raw meats. He took up bow and poisoned arrow with them, hunting labba and bush-hog. When the game was scarce he scavenged with them for skels, worms, rats, whatever lurked in holes in the ground. And when he tired of the degradation of their lives he abandoned the bush-people and returned to the haven of the estate, where there was rum and where the flesh of woman was, to his mind, less rank in smell, less coarse in texture.

He took his punishment from Gladstone and then settled down to a period of work. He entered Miriam's hut and assumed his previous space, without permission. He organised her brothers into a gang, making Thomas shave his head and scarify his face to show his African roots. He taught them coolie words – all obscene – since they had lost their original language. Under his strict supervision they practised throwing knives at young coconuts until the blade stuck first time. They exercised by climbing and re-climbing trees to pick more coconuts. When he felt they were prepared – devoted to him in body and mind – he let them loose at night to steal wood from the fence surrounding the Great House or tools from the warehouse. With the money from the sale, less a percentage for the boys, he disappeared to nigger villages along the coast to make sport. Miriam was glad to see him go for she was secretly afraid of him. He loved her only because she belonged to Gladstone. She could tell from the way he insisted on taking her at night to the cemetery, always beside or on top of old Mr Gladstone's grave. He would turn her around and press her against the cold surface, deliberately, so that she would cry out. He took pleasure in bruising her skin against the stone. She could so easily shove him off for she was stronger than him, but she permitted it. One night, in unfulfilled rage, he would go too far and close his hands around her neck – she knew it would happen for he tested her tolerance by gradual degrees. And when it happened she would knock him to the ground coarsely as she had once turned on Gladstone, leaving him sprawling at the foot of his couch, utterly terrified by what else she might do. She had stood above Gladstone, both hands behind her back as if concealing a weapon. He had looked up at her, not knowing whether to command her or to negotiate for his safety. She had reached down, plucked him up, laid him on the couch again, and left him there to regain his authority whilst considering the nature of her services.

'She die of childbirth for true, why I should lie to you?' Miriam asserted. But Rohini was too agitated to listen.

'You only say that to frighten me.'

'Frighten you? What you can do me that I should frighten you? You own money? Your bubby bigger than my own? You get more strength than me to beat me? Look at you! You so fine you can pass through needle-eye quicker than cotton thread.'

'You get your eye on Vidia, I believe so,' Rohini lied.

'Vidia? Vidia?' Miriam gathered the saliva contemptuously in her mouth but decided not to spit, to save hurting Rohini. 'Girl, I don't intend hustle Vidia, I does only go for bigness and badness,' she said reassuringly, even though it meant speaking demeaningly of herself.

The tactic backfired. Rohini was insulted. 'You think I marry mumu or what? Just because Vidia talk soft and work hard don't mean he can't box you in the face.'

Miriam looked at the swelling still evident under Rohini's eyes. She could so easily ridicule the girl and dismiss her from the cemetery but instead she drew Rohini to her gentle hug. 'Let we forgo quarrel,' she said.

And Rohini, remembering all the small ways in which Miriam had cared for her, as Finee would have done if she had been in Guiana, yielded. 'Is only because I been hoping for baby but none coming,' Rohini confessed.

'I know. I know.'

'How you know?'

'Because I live among coolie all my life and I see that if new wife don't bear within two-three year, is regular licks she getting from the man.'

'You think I will get baby one day?'

'You does do everything you need to get baby?'

'Sure,' Rohini replied, wanting to explain everything in case she was missing out some activity, but she was too shy to do so.

'The baby will come.'

Rohini believed her. After all Miriam must have slept with several men, as Vidia said all nigger women did. Miriam behaved with such vulgarity that Vidia must be right, even though in the two years of working with her she had never mentioned men, except Kampta and Gladstone. And even then she spoke of the two of them as if they were warring brothers in her care – her duty was to protect a wicked Kampta from the proper wrath of Gladstone. 'How come you get thirty years and never make baby?' Rohini ventured, wondering whether nigger women chewed on their own kumari seeds or else worked their muscles in such a way that the milk from a man couldn't squirt out.

Because they take you from behind. Because they lash you so you can bray, which is the only noise they want to hear. Because they feed in the trough between your breasts or in the trough of your mouth. Because nigger woman is her back-end.

The question hurt Miriam but she recovered instantly, a trick of self-protection practised over the years. 'I throw away enough baby in my time,' she lied. She laughed when Rohini appeared shocked, grabbed her hand and led her briskly through the graves. 'You don't want hear *my* story when so much stories lying here you have to learn.' She paused before old Gladstone's tomb, and read the epitaph aloud to Rohini, skipping over all the big words so that the inscription made no sense.

'It say Ramayana anywhere?' Rohini wanted to know, peering ignorantly at the stone.

'Ramayana? What name so?'

'Is we word. Recruiter swear this Plantation is holy place, gold bury everywhere.'

'Girl, gold bury here for truth. Old Gladstone was fat as a galleon when he was alive.' Rohini looked at her stupidly. 'Never mind galleon. You is right when you say holy, because once upon a time no holier man than old Gladstone exist in the colony. Mrs Gladstone belly only pan-boil poison. Year after year she dropping still-born child, till one year she dead out herself. They left

100

the baby inside to ferment, but two days pass and, though they rub rum in her skin to cure it, she still loosen and smell, and the baby still not coming. So they had to bury her and child – what everybody say was the only boy old Gladstone make. And old Gladstone change. He turn religious. Day and night the man repenting sin. As if he believe *he* kill the woman. Greed did fill up his eye, and gold litter his counting-house, but God didn't give what he demand, which is child. Preacherman say God does give and take away but God smart old Gladstone. God take what he didn't even give. God wicked, eh? God is Kampta self!' She roared in her usual raucous manner, gathered the spit she had intended for Rohini and aimed it at old Gladstone. 'He dead out in 1834,' she said, watching the saliva trickle down the date carved on the gravestone. 'You know how many days I stand here and spit? And I hit 1834 every time, no matter if I stand back two foot or three foot. God's brute arrow of judgement shoot from my mouth, I tell Kampta. He keep missing. He stand just here but his spit like it seek learning, it only fall sweetly on the Latin, on the opus and so-an-so puss, and whatever else nastiness write there.'

1834. A lucky year for niggers, Vidia had declared, because the 1 minus from 8 and the 3 plus the 4 made 7. And if you multiplied the 1 and the 3, and the 8 and the 4, and counted all up, you still got a number that 7 could go into. And if you took the first and the last and multiplied them, and the second and the third and multiplied them, and then added up, 7 could still go into the sum. So all in all, add or subtract or divide or multiply, the niggers lucky bad! That was the year the whiteman in England let them loose, Vidia told Rohini. Slavery end that very year and whiteman start bringing in coolie from India. And two years later, in 1836, *he* born – born to replace nigger and prosper on the plantation by sheer work. He hear story what nigger say about old Gladstone: that old Gladstone turn stupid with grieving when his wife die, and take all the nigger slaves backdam and kill them. Some say it was madness, others say he already loose his wife so he thinking why he should not loose his slaves too. So he chain them and lead them backdam and line them up and stuff cloth in their mouths to stop them begging mercy and bam! bam! bam! story done.

Then he go home and swallow poison. Some say it was because he repent. He so full with repentance for how he work nigger as slave, how he refuse them water when they drop in the sun, how he only feed them pig-foot and fish-bone and weevil-soup, how one piece serge cloth each was all he provide so nigger woman walk about half-naked to breed temptation and sin, and when nigger-child come he sell it marketplace. Old Gladstone fall down before God all night and beg mercy and next day he set all the niggers free when he kill them in backdam, and then his heart and his conscience clear, for he rid himself of his wealth. When they free, then he free to die, and when they all get to whiteman heaven, he will embrace all of them like how everybody now equal, and forgive them for lazing and fucking and thieving and pretending sickness to shirk work. But how come whiteman so foolish, Vidia asked Rohini, to let nigger cheat him year on year, and then he still forgive them? If it was he, Vidia, you would see different story! *He* kill out all his niggers? Never! He might as well kill out his cows, if he own any.

Rohini listened wearily as he babbled on, nodding agreement even when he came to the cows. She no longer cared whether or not he hit her. Even if he did he would avoid damage to her belly. He talked and talked about old Gladstone, calculating the man's fortune and weighing up how much of it was lost, how much of it could have survived and thrived had *he* been given management of it. She knew that he, like Miriam, was ignorant about old Gladstone's purpose. It was neither greed nor guilt which motivated old Gladstone but the *idea* of endeavour, the *idea* of making a structure in the bush. Plantation Albion was a single factory with only so many thousand acres of cane, but whole continents were drawn into its creation – slaves from Africa, coolies from India, managers from England, tools from America. The whiteman had stitched the world together with beautiful embroidery, differently coloured threads joining differently coloured countries to make a priceless tapestry. The ships came and went, ferrying sugar, tobacco, spices, cloth and machinery from all corners of the globe. Even the ships themselves were crafted in Malabar teak, Irish oak, American mahogany, though they wore the flag of only one country. Rohini didn't have all such details at hand but looking out from the kitchen window of the Great House at the endless fields she knew she was in the midst of a great enterprise. In India, when she surveyed the land from Droopatie's verandah, what did she see but a litter of straw-topped huts? In her province there were thousands of villages and millions of people, but the size of the place didn't inspire reverence. Its size could not overcome its shabbiness, its haphazardness, and the population laboured piecemeal with nothing but sticks or hoes in their hands. When they set off from their village to Calcutta, she expected to encounter wonderful scenes. But the villages along the way milled with people like themselves – scrawny, bare-footed, unfinished, with a look of unreal expectancy in their eyes. Here in Guiana, they were put to work, but it was work which gave them a place in the progress of the world – the factory and the sugar it made were the future, not cow-milk and handspun cotton. But the coolies were ungrateful, harbouring their coins or threatening to strike for more, as if all that mattered was the money. They measured their work by their wages, not by the idea of a priceless tapestry that old Gladstone wanted to involve them in. He must have suffered, not only because he was far from England and its comforts and finery, but out of loneliness. He must have suffered, having to nurture the idea within himself, no one understanding his purpose, not even his wife. A son, perhaps, could inherit and further Old Gladstone's mission of imposing order in the bush, but his wife disappointed him, as his niggers did. He beat the niggers as frustratedly as he made love to his wife but none of them was productive. When she died, he rid himself of the idea by ridding himself of the slaves. He took them to the backdam to be killed, for they belonged to the bush. They were incapable of order, so he let them loose. The bush was victorious. When he died, the bush would return to overrun the Plantation he had redeemed from it.

Rohini couldn't express it but when she stood before his grave she could sense the nature of his suffering. The cemetery was festooned with graves, each bordered with shrubs and flowers to form a pleasing pattern. Each grave was laid out purposefully, husband alongside wife, with the children neatly clustered around them; the size of each grave reflected the rank and status of its occupant. It was the order old Gladstone desired in life but could only experience in death. The very permanence of the stone proclaimed his everlasting failure. Old Gladstone's headpiece had writing on it, but there was space in the corners. She wished she could write, then she could use that space to tell his story fully. As it was, Miriam lied about what was inscribed there, converting the Latin into nigger words so as to degrade him. *Miriam* was the bush that would overrun even the most sacred of places, choke the most sacred of expressions.

'The year old Gladstone dead in 1834 all we black folk set free. Grandpa tell me how we mash down the road with dance! And tumble up in bed! Woman bear baby non-stop the next year, like is the black plague grip Guiana. Everywhere, whiteman flee the country from we disease or hide in their house and cock their gun.'

'Plenty people kill that year?' Rohini asked, pausing from her work at the mention of guns.

Miriam reached and plucked some bananas from a bunch hanging from the ceiling. She prodded them to make sure they were sufficiently ripe, unpeeled one and gave it to Rohini. 'Girl, stop fussing, nuh? All day you scraping and scrubbing Gladstone house as if it belong to you.' Gladstone was away on business for a few days but Rohini only doubled her cleaning efforts. She would not betray him like the rest of them. As soon as his back was turned some took ill and queued up outside the dispensary. Others lay down cutlass to throw dice or suck at a rum-bottle. She wished she could look Gladstone in the face and tell him what scamps he had for a workforce, but the idea of speaking her thoughts to him, much less raising her eyes to meet his, was unthinkable.

'Come we go thief from Gladstone room,' Miriam giggled, snatching the cloth from Rohini's hand and flinging it to the floor.

'Thief? You mad or what?' Rohini said, reaching to pick up the cloth.

'Leave that cloth alone,' Miriam boomed with such force that Rohini froze. She bullied the girl out of the kitchen and upstairs to Gladstone's study. A huge iron safe dominated the room. Miriam stepped on a chair, ran her hand along the ceiling's ledge and located the key. 'We does bury thing but whitepeople does hide them high, nearer to God, where pagan hand can't reach,' she said triumphantly, stepping down from the chair. 'Sometimes I think if I search all the rafters and roofspace in this house, diamonds wrap in cobweb I will harvest, which whiteman forget he save there. Christian people got no shame! They dead out and leave not one cent to a grateful nigger. The money bundle up on high like if it is church collection to fill God-eye and buy salvation, like if salvation is just another nigger.' She turned the handle and pulled with all her might, her face contorting with all the effort. Afterwards she sat before the open safe to catch her breath, fanning herself violently with an old will taken from among the bundles of estate papers.

'Is beating we get from Gladstone if he find out,' Rohini whispered, yet surrendering to curiosity and poking her head into the safe.

'The Last Will and Testament of Joseph Countryman, 1812,' Miriam read aloud, and with much concentration. She fanned herself again and sneezed over the document. She wiped it as best she could at the side of her dress and thrust it at Rohini. 'Put this whiteman back in the bundle and pass me somebody else with less dust.' Rohini took the will between thumb and forefinger, avoiding the smears. She dropped it on the nearest pile of papers, not caring whether it was out of place. 'The one next to the inkwell,' Miriam ordered, directing Rohini to the second shelf. The document was wrapped in a bright red ribbon and the paper was freshly white, not stiff and mottled like the others. 'This here is Mrs Aldrington, my favourite,' Miriam grinned, unpicking the ribbon, 'she does give the best, like sea breeze. Less than five years now she depart this life.'

'You knows the woman?' Rohini asked, alarmed at the way Miriam whipped the paper before her face and settled back in the chair contentedly, without the least sign of fear.

'Know? Of course I knows her. Why else you think I choose her from the safe above all the rest? When she been living in the same room here that Gladstone turn into a study, me did serve her.'

'This same room here?'

106

'Just where you standing she used to catch the light from the window.' When Rohini shifted predictably Miriam laughed. 'She was harmless like you, how she can haunt? You so skinny your ghost hardly will get shape. Just so she stay.'

'But you believe all whitepeople evil, not so?' Rohini asked in a hushed voice, not wanting to provoke Mrs Aldrington.

'Not she. When old Gladstone die without child the estate inherit by his nephew, Mr Gladstone, who was orphan boy in England and Mrs Aldrington travel with him as guardian. She look after him well till my time come.' She fanned the air and sniffed as if to catch a trace of Mrs Aldrington. 'Sea-breeze. Come smell and tell me.'

Rohini leant forwards and breathed in the saltiness of Miriam's sweat. 'Strong sea-breeze, eh?' Miriam beamed as Rohini stepped back and shuddered inwardly. 'The woman love the sea more than she love man. In England she had beach-house and she tell me about cliff and cockle and seagull which give her sweet companionship after her husband perish in Africa. Whitepeople funny bad, some of them does prefer to live with fish than man!'

'Let we close the safe and go downstairs,' Rohini urged, not wanting to be party to Miriam's abuse of Gladstone's people and possessions.

'Still, Mrs Aldrington was kind,' Miriam continued, ignoring her. 'Her husband went to trade in Africa and a nigger throw a spear that bore through his eyeball and lodge in his brain, but she never beat me once, never. She managed the estate till Gladstone grow up, and give proper pay to workers. She got no interest in the money, all she want is sea. But how she hate Demerara sea! Mud-brown, and shark in the water, and dead niggers wash up on the beach from other plantations. She hate Guiana. She used to run her hand between my plaits and mutter, as if the lice and oil and mat and black partings remind her of Guiana, but still she never beat. Instead she tell me about England, how she used to sit on the beach under a broad umbrella and watch the rain nipping the sea, the drizzle fine and English, and the sea licking its skin to smooth it where the rain ruffle it, and all day rain and sea playing and teasing each other like English kittens. Is not sex she did want but sea and drizzle, but all she get in Guiana is a beach where the water lash and pound, and not far out from shore a shark snatching at some dead body.'

Miriam searched the safe but took away a mere coin. She was not interested in stealing from Gladstone. The coin was a token of the fact that she was free to do so. The freedom was more valuable than the coin. 'If I ask him he would give ten coin but I'd rather thief. He thief it from me in the first place, from my Ma and Pa and grandpa and all the niggers who old Gladstone murder, so how he can give what don't belong to him?'

Rohini agreed, to keep the peace. Miriam was in an angry mood. The memory of Mrs Aldrington's kindness seemed to provoke resentment in her. 'I was a girl then, and when she play with my hair I miss my mother. But how an old, grey-skinned English bitch like that can be *my* mother?' She tied the ribbon tightly around the will, as if it were a noose. She tossed the lot into the safe, braced her back against the door and slammed it shut.

When they returned to the kitchen Miriam plucked two bananas and stuffed them into her mouth to contain her rage. She chewed and swallowed what she could, then spat the rest on the floor. 'Clean it!' she commanded.

'Man, Miriam, why you behaving so?' Rohini protested.

Because I fat and my bubby full and I submit and roll my eyes and gurgle like nigger-maid. Because is 1860 but wait till 1960, one hundred years, when I grow slim like Gladstone book and full of words like grandpa, and who will force me to scrub floor then, wash clothes, cook, take cock, when I have freedom? Till that time come, I play nigger, I breed fear.'

'Clean it!' Miriam bellowed and this time Rohini automatically reached for the cloth. 'If whiteman order, you run fast-fast to serve. But nigger is nothing, eh? I is nothing?' She stared accusingly at the girl. 'Don't think I don't realise that all-you coolie people come to Guiana to enslave we. And everything we build up, all the dams and all the canals we dig and all the cane we plant, you people greed for and conspire to inherit.'

'I come to work, not ride on your back. I never even knew nigger live in Guiana,' Rohini replied, wanting to be friends again but Miriam would not be placated. She watched sternly as Rohini wiped up her spittle. *She* was Gladstone's maid. Rohini was only a minor servant. 'Soon you will eye-pass me and answer back. You will conspire to gather up Gladstone and all his gifts,' Miriam shouted after Rohini as she withdrew to the sink to rinse the cloth. It was only when Miriam saw her body convulse that she relented. She threw a banana in Rohini's direction. The banana fell into the sink and Rohini stared at it. 'Eat, you maga-rass coolie,' she ordered, hoping that her bullying tone would stun the girl and prevent her from crying. She went and stood beside her, wanting to comfort her but not knowing how. 'Give me the cloth,' she said, snatching it from her hand and elbowing her away from the sink. 'Who give you authority to scrub my spit? You think you can become nigger overnight? You think you can just step off the ship and start polishing people backside and prune people toe-nail? You know how long it take *me* to grow so fat and sly and foul-mouth and thieving and top kitchen-and-bedroom servant and the bestest grinning willing hymn-singing nigger in this kiss-me-arse crab-louse colony?' She prodded a fat finger into Rohini's chest to punctuate her question. 'You cry, and practise crying if you want to become top-servant and take over from me. Because when Gladstone stroke your front sweetly and when he turn you round and put thing in your back, is two different kind of crying you got to do. You already cry before Gladstone when Vidia beat you, so you done make a good start.'

You break the back of a cockroach with a full blow of your pointer-broom, then flick it to one side and continue sweeping. When all things shining in Gladstone room, the shelves scrape and the things on it straighten, the bedsheet freshly spread, you slouch in his chair to watch your handiwork, looking around at the silverware and leather you done polish, the books and papers tidy up, the wardrobe of clothes wash and starch and press, when a movement break your eye's satisfaction. The cockroach, the blasted coolie, stir and slide along its squashed belly, slide on its own slime and kicking with what legs left towards the nearest ledge, the nearest space of dust and cobweb which you neglect to clean, the nearest darkness, to lay. So coolie stay. So nigger Miriam stay. You beat and humiliate but still they spawn and will overrun. One day, this clean room, this cemetery, this canefield and everything Gladstone and his forebears construct, will turn bush. Coolie and nigger will run through the estate with torch to burn down the factory and house (Rohini could see it), massacring the horses and mules and Gladstone, and famine will follow, but they too gleeful to mind, once Gladstone lie bleeding over his possessions. Freedom is a word, freedom is belly-wind, yet is freedom they will starve for. Kumar was same like them. He want nothing because that is all he is, and he lie to Vidia. He claim he bury money but is the seeds of nothing he sow in the ground, nigger-weed, that's all.

Rohini could see it as clearly as she could see her reflection in the table. She squirted some more wax on the wood and daubed it over the surface to disfigure her appearance. 'I must speak to him,' she said, polishing the table to recover her image. 'What you say? you think I should warn Gladstone?' She looked sternly at herself, as if awaiting wise advice. 'Well, speak girl, don't fear that my hand swipe your mouth.' 'I knows, Mr Gladstone. You does treat man like rotten tooth that you yank and spit from your mouth, but we ladies is confectionery.' She glanced away, not daring to look at herself, out of shyness. 'How coolie like you know word like confectionery?' she interrogated herself in a voice tinged with anger. 'One hundred other big words and more I can know,' she replied, choosing to defy the warning. She laughed his laugh, a dry, joyless sound she had heard him make whenever whiteman Fielding from the neighbouring estate came to visit. They sat opposite each other, smoking pipes, talking about politics in England, wars in Europe, and other big matters. If she listened hard outside the door she could sense the seriousness in their voices and follow some of their conversation. They spoke of countries called France and Spain, and of the threat to English trade. They spoke of a people called the Irish, and their voices suddenly became agitated. It was when they discussed their own estates, complaining about rising costs, falling sales, unwilling and ungrateful workers, that Gladstone laughed, a nervous, dangerous laugh like that a man makes to himself when plotting mischief.

And now he was staring at her, making the same laugh, but she was not afraid. She could stop him with a swish of her cloth, as his uncle took the blade to nigger throats, as she put her hand over Vidia's mouth to stop his silly sex noises. 'You think you can fill my mouth with your confectionery and do nastiness inside me and afterwards give me empty glass jar and tin-can with English picture paint on it like you do Miriam? You think you can dig me up, put something inside me secretly, then bury me again so that no one can catch you and bring shame on your name? You think I can satisfy with a small piece here and a favour there?' She held the tube of wax over his face, ready to squeeze some into his eyes. He looked alarmed and moved to one side, but she shifted her head and brought him again to the centre of the table. 'What you want then, what I must give you?' She made him plead and struggle to escape, but she fixed him to the wood as he had so frequently fixed Kampta to the star-apple tree. 'You want me to blind you? You want me to make it so that when you wake up in the morning and look out of your window your wide fields

111

disappear, the huge factory, the tall chimney?' 'What I must give you?' he repeated, his voice hoarse with terror. 'You. Is you I want to own like tin-can. Miriam does spit and piss in your tin-can and glass-jar for spite but I can put in coolie confectionery. I can dip my hand in white-sugar bowl and hold it over your face and circle, like blessings, like bangles of light.' She viewed his face as it tilted towards hers, surrendering to her promise. 'Give up Miriam,' she ordered, and he withdrew instinctively as if slapped into cowardice. 'You is a born fool to let Miriam bully you, you weaker than all the niggers and coolies who serve you,' she chided him. 'But Miriam is my maid, she do what *I* tell her,' he protested feebly. 'She do what *she* do,' Rohini said curtly. There was an embarrassed silence, Gladstone stunned by the shame of having been discovered, and Rohini suddenly becoming afraid to speak what she had witnessed. She spread the cloth over the table to cover his face, and hers, took up her pointer-broom and followed the cockroach's trail to resume her killing.

Gladstone's bedroom was the only space in the plantation where Rohini felt privileged, marked out from the misery of her coolie status. She moved among his possessions as if they belonged to her. The silk, the silver, the curios, the leather-clad books were hers to pick up, examine, dust down, breathe upon intimately, rub, replace. She removed the hairs carefully from Gladstone's ivory comb. They were threads of gold and she saved the longest for her needle. One day she would stitch a tear in her sari with them, to remember her time among ugly men in an ugly land. The coolies gossiped about her lack of child, spreading malice about Vidia's manhood. They would breed her if they were given her, but even this threat to his marriage seemed to go unnoticed for Vidia was immersed in his work. He no longer kept a check on her comings and goings from Gladstone's house, contented with the sum of her wages which relieved him of having to spend some of his own money on their upkeep. When Gladstone entertained overnight and Rohini asked to stay over, he made the most perfunctory of protests before allowing it. Still, he asked after her comfort, insisting that she take their only blanket to Gladstone's house to keep herself warm on the kitchen floor where she slept. He would make do with some cloth wrapped around his legs and the heat from the oil-lamp. He enquired after her tasks in the Great House, listened sadly as she detailed them. His pity angered her, and his reassurances that soon, when he had accumulated enough, she would be relieved of the drudgery. He would build a house, and seek promotion to wages clerk, given that he was the best coolie at counting. He would earn more, to maintain the house and to send her to the missionary school where she could learn to read and recite. Their children would not be like them, but would grow up to get the best jobs on the estate, in the accounts department, sitting at a desk beside whitepeople.

All this she wanted, especially the learning of English, but still she resented the freedom he was giving her, the freedom to work in Gladstone's house at whatever hours he demanded. She wanted Vidia to be fierce in his distrust and to supervise her doings with a vigilant and suspicious eye. And yet, it was exactly such restraint that made her kill the cow and flee from India. But even in India, Vidia was irrationally trustful, leaving her in the company of his father. She would be safe in his father's house, safe from the ambitions of other men, so he believed. That was the way things had always been done in India, and he conformed to ritual as obediently as his goats ran before him each morning to a familiar field. Perhaps what provoked her was neither freedom nor bondage but the pettiness of both. In their village, what was freedom but your own pot and pan, and what was bondage but your breasts tapering to the suction of your husband's mouth? Here in the plantation, freedom and bondage were big ideas. She couldn't speak them, not knowing the words, but they had to do with war upon the blacks, war upon the bush. And it was war she wanted, not the normal ascent from bare-handed coolie to coolie-with-hut, which Vidia plotted; big war, which even though it brought cruelty, such as old Mr Gladstone's slaying of the niggers, also brought change. And what would life be like without change but the life she led in India, day dropping dully upon day, and when it was all over some mildewed hand corking the bottle and burying her away forever?

She ran her hand through the ruffles of Gladstone's shirt for the sensation of its whiteness and cleanliness. She liked the feel of his velvet tunic with its bright, engraved buttons. His wardrobe was packed with special clothes belonging only to whitepeople, some decorated with embroidery and other curious patterns. She examined a badge sewn on one of his jackets. Why was it there? No doubt some honour he win for his country. Missie Queen self sew it on with pure gold needle, one million thousand stinking coolie rupees can't even buy needle like that. Whitepeople born different, eh? Look how they change the world and rule all over India. The greatest maharajah with all his treasure and silk and lace around his neck and ornament pin in his shirt still can't gleam like one single Gladstone whiteman. Or like Missie Queen Victoria needle. If only she own such needle to thread his hairs into her sari. But it would take three or four or five lifetimes of scraping to buy one. 'Next time I born, Lord Jesus willing…' and she knelt and proceeded to scrub, drawn back to the commonness of her own being but glad to be in his service, close to his things, close to the big ideas which changed things, even though they brought whipping and burning and death and slavery for some. And she was glad she killed the cow and broke from the village gods. Vidia stopped beating her for this. Even he must have realised that she had sacrificed all for the sake of his own progress, even though he remained a small-minded coolie, measuring his worth in one-two jars of coin.

'So what you bring me this time?' Kampta snarled as soon as Miriam approached the hut. It was past midnight. He had stayed awake to greet her, fretting and cursing all the six hours Gladstone delayed her. She was exhausted, she wanted to bathe and sleep, not engage with his anger, but he would not let her. He looked contemptuously upon the parcel of salted ham she handed over as if it were meagre booty. 'You mean you skin your back-end all night for a piece of ham?' he asked in mock disbelief, treating her with the same scorn he heaped upon her brothers when they returned from their nightly expeditions with only a pocketful of nails. He made them feel guilty for having betrayed him and their forebears. He had trained them physically, had tutored them with stories to provoke their sense of hurt and rage, and when the moment was perfect, he released them on a raiding mission. But all they brought back were weak excuses. 'I don't care if Gladstone put two or twelve extra night-watchman to guard factory,' he screamed at them, 'all-you just useless. When Gladstone land in Africa he raid enough to pack one hundred thousand shiploads, and all he had was one gun. You hear, one gun. And you know what else he had?' He threw the question at Thomas who looked away in shame. 'Brains. The man had brains. Brains is what most people carry in their heads but all-you head stuff with blood-cloth.' They fidgeted, the nails bulging in their pockets and digging into their flesh. They had walked the two miles from the factory in pain, but Kampta made them wait a little longer before allowing them to empty their pockets.

'Next time he open his coolie mouth at me I kill his rass,' Thomas told his brothers when Kampta was far away. But he knew that it was an empty threat, even though he had grown to the size of a young balata tree, his skin rough and uneven as bark, hair branching wildly around his head. He knew that Kampta was right to shout, for what was a shilling worth of nails compared to the money Gladstone was making from all of them.

'You have to thief and wreck and laze and fuck and drink and knock drum and make song that mock Gladstone, for soon your life done but *he* still own your legacy,' Kampta had preached to them. 'Remember your grandpappy them, black and angry though they weak with lash and two-three teeth only left in their mouth how they break the rest against sheep-bone and what-else bone whiteman feed them. Two-three teeth in their mouth like when goat enter cornfield and eat out corn and two-three ears only hanging from the husk. Is so whiteman eat out your grandpappy but even so, is rebellion they perform, and burn down canefield, and sharpen their teeth against whiteman, and sing Christian song in his ears till he surrender.'

Sleep. She wanted sleep, not fight, but Kampta would not let her go.

'A piece of ham?' he repeated but still she did not answer. 'You mean the man heap up gold in his house but all you take is ham?'

'It come all the way from England,' she offered, for want of something better to say.

'England? England?' Kampta repeated quietly, turning his face to the darkness as if to better visualise the country. 'So you let him, in return for a slice of England?' The quietness of his voice made her fear him. She could cope with him when he ranted or preached, knowing that as long as she listened sympathetically his anger would subside. But she had also seen him talking to himself in a low voice as he paced the ruined garden – he had forbidden her brothers to plant, for planting was slavery – and she knew that he was pitchforking in his mind the nastiest of manure. He was frustrated. He had only an army of three boys at his disposal, insufficient for all the deeds of revenge his mind dreamt up. In such a mood she avoided him, making excuses to visit relatives in the neighbouring village which took her away for a whole day. But there was no escape now. Her thighs hurt from Gladstone's doing so even if she wanted to run away into the bush she could not. Best to look abject. Best to cry, to disarm him. Best to limp away, crying. In the morning, after a full night's rest, she could fight him. She could chase him from her yard for the hundredth time. She could taunt him for being a good-for-nothing, abandoned coolie drowning in self-pity. She could order her brothers back to the garden. But not now. Not when he spoke quietly. She could feel real tears gathering, not feigned, as she planned, but from real fear. With Gladstone she acted, squealing or weeping according to the role he chose for her. Sometimes she would confuse the masks of brazenness or terror so as to spoil his fantasies and leave him unfinished. But mostly she complied, for fear of her domestic wages which fed and clothed her brothers, with a portion put aside each week for her mother, when she returned.

'So everytime you lie with Gladstone, is England you lying with? When he heave on top of you is a whole country, great and heavy, pressing down on you so you can't escape?' He let the ham drop from his hands as if to free them for some deed. 'But Miriam girl, tell truth,' he said playfully, almost with a small boy's innocence, 'you like England, no? When he put it in, you does close your eye and imagine you is whitelady riding through mist and meadow and all them other pictures paint on all the tin-cans he give you? You does open and close like how whitewoman does do her umbrella when the fine rain fall then sun come out?'

Is spit I get, not gentle rain and breeze, she wanted to answer, a middle-age man rising and falling and fanning me with his flab, and he so excited he fart and dribble, and by the time he finish my whole face wet with spit and the bed smelling of horse-manure. This is what I do for all-you ungrateful dogs, she wanted to say, and is my mother make me do it. When she come back she will want finery or else she will run away again... and if she run away again I burn the hut with Thomas and Joe and Peter sleeping in it, and I sprinkle white spirit over my head and light it, and I run through the canefield torching till I reach Gladstone's house. But if by that time the flame on my skin is low, then I go stoop and blow on my foot, blow steadfast till no breath left, till the flame start up and find fresh fuel underneath my skin and lick the whole of my body; then I stroll from room to room setting them afire. Stoop and blow, and not make one noise, not one scream, like I stoop now quietly at your foot to pick up my ham, pick it up and

117

dust if off, like I pick up myself from Gladstone bed and brush off the flakes of his skin. Like the preacherman break bread over my head and the white crumbs sprinkle in my hair and kindle and it become burning bush and I hear God denouncing me, *me*, from above, for sinning and how *I* must seek forgiveness. Like you standing over me now, raging with fire inside you which you want to put in me, purify me, and me kneeling as at church-altar, but is not blessing I want but my fucking ham which I fuck for, roll in the dust for, so move your manfoot and fucking cock, you and God and Gladstone, and let me pass. Let me pass, she ordered, but no word came from her mouth, only a sob which she dampened immediately for she would not cry real tears for him, nor for any of them, not even for her mother.

He, Kampta, would murder Gladstone and be free at last of the rage which clung to him like the skaps' nest on the jamoon tree. There would be chaos afterwards, an outpouring of blood as coolies ran from the bayonets of English soldiers. The Governor would despatch a small army to avenge Gladstone's death. They would execute a dozen or so coolies, as an example to the whole colony. They would rape no more than two or three women. They would burn down all the huts with all their coolie belongings. They would impose a week's curfew so that no one could venture from their charred surroundings in search of food, or wood to build new shelters. The weakest – mostly the elderly, the useless – would die of malnutrition and the cold. Magistrates would be despatched to try the guilty, sentencing half a dozen ringleaders to be hanged, and the same number of accomplices to a lifetime of labour in the nearest malarial swamp. A few months later a Commission of Enquiry would be set up, comprising learned men from England and respectable whitepeople from the colony. The punishment would be done this way, Kampta knew from the accounts he had heard of slave uprisings from the older niggers. When the first rebellion occurred in the previous century, the English slaughtered five hundred slaves. The bloodiness of the massacre shocked both sides. The slave became aware of their power to damage the psyche of the English by their monumental acts of sacrifice. The English instituted a Commission of Enquiry to find ways of minimising the loss of slave lives and the loss to the economy, as well as the brutalisation of the common soldiers. One day the soldier was a pig-farmer's son from a Norfolk village, accustomed only to the innocence of the abattoir. The next day, despatched to quell rebellion in the colony, he disembowelled women with finesse, with a few expert thrusts of his bayonet. Such evolution could not be tolerated for it represented a threat to England itself. The soldier would eventually return home with the habits of a spontaneous brute. The crime and disorder of the colony, which he carried with him like a virus, would sicken England. Something had to be done to restrain colonial passions to the proportions of a civilised Englishness. At the next rebellion the soldiers were sent in with rationed bullets. Fewer slaves died. After the hangings, the resulting Commission of Enquiry conceded an hour a month for attending church or an extra ladle of plantains and pig-foot soup. The enslaved Africans exhausted their new privileges and rioted again. This time the Commission allowed their leaders to speak, five extra yards of serge cloth and a holiday on Good Friday to add to their Christmas Day break. Rebellions broke out periodically, but the enslaved Africans mixed peaceful Christian protest, headed by recognised church leaders, with acts of sabotage carried out by select warriors. The English shot at the warriors and negotiated with the Christians. Over the decades leading up to 1834, there was less and less need for bullets and more and more privileges guaranteed on paper so that when freedom came, the Africans and the English had achieved a fragile order based on a truce on unnecessary bloodletting.

Kampta knew, from listening to the stories of the older niggers of how they wore their masters down, that the English soldiers would have no stomach for massacre, that they had long lost the instinct for wanton maiming and raping. These days the English ruled by the whip, knowing that the weals would eventually heal. They rule by money, paying each coolie a wage, making him believe that more would be forthcoming with time. And they set up the odd school, to give the coolie English words, to link education with reward, so that the coolie believed that his illiteracy and ignorance were the cause of his backwardness. It took over a century to acquire freedom and it would take another century to acquire the education that made Gladstone economically superior to him. The coolie must work harder, he must sacrifice, he must endure, he must wait.

Wait scunt! Kampta would not wait. Wait till Gladstone eat out all of Miriam and blight her with whiteman germ so she spoil for all time? No, kill whiteman now! A handful of coolies would die, but it is time coolie learn what nigger gone through. Coolie come here thinking the bush clear by itself and nobody plant the fields and miracle dig the canals, but miracle is nigger, and all the canal-water pool together is one drop compared to all the nigger sweat. When English kill a few, then coolie will know the truth that each penny Gladstone pay them make from the same metal as the bullet that bore into nigger backside long-time. But no, they bow down and kiss his foot, bare their back for Gladstone to chastise whilst woman widen to take different lash. He go kill Gladstone for Miriam's sake. If he had to explain it he use foul speech that make her out to be only her pokey-hole, because he don't have the fancy words to describe her. But he, Kampta, had deep feelings for Miriam, but he wouldn't dwell on them because he would get stupid with grief and wander the plantation like madman, children chasing him and pelting stone. And he would grow weak because he lose his appetite and sicken and become useless like the niggers freshly landed from Africa pining for family and familiar place, refusing food, knocking their head with stone, crying so much that all the salt remove from their blood which turn thin and watery and seep from their arsehole in constant diarrhoea till they keel over dead. No, he Kampta would chew on foul words to maintain himself bitter and gather strength to kill Gladstone. Miriam understand. She does curse him back, matching foul word with foul word. And even if he had fancy word he still wouldn't speak it because then the badness he wear on his face would slip and people would laugh at him, calling him blue-saki, flamingo, love-bird, when is hawk he is, hawk or harpy pecking at itself to rouse the cancer clinging there.

But perhaps it was not Gladstone he hated but himself, Kampta thought, hiding in the area of bush where Gladstone usually came to hunt. Kampta would wait for him to return with an empty gun. As Gladstone rested on a rock, admiring his catch, Kampta would startle him with a raised cutlass. It was an ill-conceived plan. He should have prepared his attack more conscientiously. He should have reconnoitred the area of bush beforehand, noticing whether any niggers grazed their sheep there in case someone spied him in the act. He should have sharpened his cutlass to minimise the mess. A dull blade meant a longer time in the killing. As it was he left everything to the moment. In the middle of a day's work he took up his cutlass and abandoned the canefield without giving a plausible explanation to anyone. He took the most visible route out of the compound, sauntering down the dam that led to the hunting ground, waving his cutlass to greet the boys casting nets into the canal. The alertness and secrecy he taught Miriam's brothers he now disregarded. When the Commission of Enquiry was set up, the cane cutters would say they were suspicious when he left work unexpectedly; the boys fishing the canal would be witnesses to the direction he took that day. But he didn't care – he would be beyond the reach of the English, in some Amerindian village-clearing in the heart of the Guiana jungle, with Miriam and her brothers.

An hour later, enveloped by bush, mosquitoes biting everywhere, inside his ears, inside his nostrils, and his quarter of rum nearly drained, Kampta doubted his mission. What Gladstone do to him to deserve death? He didn't ask to born whiteman, just as Kampta didn't ask to born a base coolie. He was only orphan boy when they remove him from England and make him proprietor of the plantation. The place got to run perfect, the factory machine demand cane, the cane demand cutlass, the cutlass demand black hand. Nigger, coolie, cane, bagasse, punt, mule, molasses, sugar, rum, ship, barrel, money – all this complication whiteman in control of, day and night, till he drop with fatigue or from some ungrateful blade at his neck. And so what if he want piece of Miriam's sugar-cake for his troubles? So what if Miriam want give? Who know if Gladstone don't love her equal to what he hate her, and who know if she don't hate him back with the same love? What matter is that the factory run perfect, and that's why coolie and nigger and whiteman got to stay clear of each other. God make things so, and you have to accept that the most that can happen is a little secret fucking in the dark and hope that God don't see you, like Gladstone doing it to Miriam late at night, when no other whiteman around to shame him, or charge him for exposing the colony to the danger of a half-caste breed, or for putting ideas into nigger people head that they beautiful – that's why whiteman desire them – so why they can't have this right and that right and more wage.

Where all this pussy business will stop? Time come and niggers get loose. Then they demand free land. Soon they will join with coolie and demand vote. Then they will want sit in Governor's house and rule the colony. All because Gladstone weak in flesh. Imagine, a piece of sugar-cake the size of his palm can change the whole course of the colony and make a nigger king, a coolie governor.

Kampta brushed the cloud of mosquitoes from his face as if clearing his mind for decision. He ran his fingers along the blunt blade of his cutlass for the umpteenth time, but before he could act Gladstone rode up. He watched Gladstone dismount and unfasten his shotgun from the side of the saddle. Then, instead of taking the path running along the edge of the jungle, Gladstone acted unexpectedly; he walked towards the patch of the bush where Kampta hid, the gun cocked. Kampta ducked, fell on his belly, and crawled away, seeking the darkness of thicker bush. He wriggled out of his half-pants and slimed through the mud to better camouflage his body. Gladstone, seeing the tops of bush waving, a tell-tale sign of a pig's stealthy escape, opened fire. A noise erupted from Kampta's mouth and he instinctively wormed his body deeper into the mud. The noise must have sounded like a terrified pig, for Gladstone halted and turned away. Today he was interested in bird, not beast. He had come to shoot toucans. He was only testing the range of his gun, and the straightness of his aim, by firing at the animal.

Kampta kept totally still, long after Gladstone's departure. Some newly-born millipedes, innocent of human spitefulness, danced up to his face, climbed upon it then scattered all over his back in infant disorder. A jena-bird hopped out of its hiding place to investigate. It stood a safe distance and looked at Kampta intently, tilting its head at all angles to get a complete view, then shaking its white beard as if in pity at the spectacle. The mud hardened to a cocoon around Kampta's body. He began to lose all sensation of fear, and with it, the desire to rise. He felt snug within the livery of mud, as if his mother had not died but was forever gathering his child's head to the garment of her body, to prevent him from seeing and hearing all the coolieness he was doomed to inherit. Enfolded in his mother, none of their doings could affect him – not the vulgar cackle of rumshop men; nor the fields freshly mutilated by their cutlasses; nor the women like so many stumps of cane after they received their beatings or their sex. But his mother had died suddenly, without warning, like the explosion of Gladstone's gun; the casing of mud shattered, and he arose and walked upright, like any man.

'I ain't no bound coolie for five-year contract. I can cut loose and leave today self,' Kampta said defiantly. There was a hollowness in his voice though which made Vidia no longer startled by his boasts and threats. Kampta sensed he had lost some esteem in the eyes of Vidia. Before, he could shock the boy with his belligerency, and gain small favours from him. Vidia would supply small measures of rum, or cut Kampta's portion of canefield whilst he slept. In return Kampta taught him how to spell the names of the tools the coolies used – cutlass, hoe, fork, shovel. One day Vidia would become the estate's accounts-clerk and he would need to maintain an inventory to prevent theft from the workers. He would win favour from Gladstone for his efforts. Vidia was glad to exchange a little rum, a little tobacco and some bundles of cane, for words which one day would make him double or triple the money he spent on Kampta.

'So where you will run this time?' Vidia asked.

Run? This time? There was the slightest trace of contempt in the way Vidia put the question. 'I don't run,' Kampta snarled, but the recollection of cowering in the mud tempered his anger. The boy had lost respect for him, in the space of a few weeks... from the time he arose from the mud, his hair matted, his penis exposed to the shrieking laughter of sakiwinki monkeys. They shook the branches overhead as he wandered through the bush, dropping bark, dead leaves, dung; from the time he resumed work the next day, borrowing a cutlass, making excuses for having lost his. He, Kampta, making excuses! The gang leader lent him one, puzzled by his politeness, for before Kampta would normally have snatched one out of the hand of the nearest smaller coolie and claimed it for his own. All day, and the next, and over the following weeks he showed up punctually, working beside them as an equal, even helping out when they struggled under the weight of cane, taking the heaviest bundles to the punts without demanding favours.

At night he lay in his section of the hut, not speaking to Miriam's brothers. They kept their silence, not daring to probe into his behaviour lest he suddenly reared up at them. A cornered animal, that is what Gladstone had turned him into. It was not the same when Gladstone had him tied to the tree. It was in the open, on the brightest of Sunday mornings, and when he looked up, there were green star-apples like a hundred whiteman – eyes to witness the deed, and kiskidees, lizards, malabuntas, everything natural living in the tree, and coolies gathered on the grass freshly cut and rinsed in dew in preparation for the beating. He felt no shame then, standing up defiantly when all expected him to drop by the fifth blow. He knew how much the coolies admired and feared him. He could take all the beatings in the world to maintain his status with them. And with Miriam who moved among them, flirting, behaving indecently, munching their dhallpuris, pretending not to be bothered, but all the time addressing him secretly to show strength, and plotting how to murder Gladstone as each lash came.

'What bad egg and louse hatching in your head?' Miriam asked as he brooded in the hut, but he waved her away, suddenly discomforted by the strength of her presence. If a hundred coolies were around he would have arisen from the bush to confront Gladstone's gun. But there was no one to witness his courage so he remained supine, like some terrified bush-animal. Gladstone had made him into a thing rising from the mud and crawling away on hands and feet; a man so less than man that even the monkeys rattled their branches and screamed in fright and amusement.

He would go back to the bush, to the Amerindian villages in the heart of the country where no whiteman trod, where he could escape from hatred and shame. 'But that is the heart of nowhere,' Vidia said, appalled by Kampta's wilfulness as he had been by Kumar's. Kampta pretended otherwise. He summoned up his cunning at story-telling to try to convince Vidia that he was not running away in defeat, but to a life more contented than a Gladstone coolie's. The Amerindians had no care for possessions. They made no marks of ownership on the land. They fished and hunted only for what they needed, not for the sport of killing. They walked the earth naked, empty-handed. The more Kampta sought to paint them in an idyllic light the more Vidia was harassed by the image of Kumar.

'Man, you talking stupidness,' Vidia said, surprised at his own boldness. He was even more surprised when Kampta, instead of staring threateningly at him, stared inwardly, brooding on the falseness and yet the promise of his tale. 'If you leave Gladstone you become less than man,' Vidia said, quietly, almost to himself, as if working out the situation he found himself in and was doomed to remain in.

'Less than man?' Kampta asked, emerging from the gloom. Vidia couldn't reason it clearly but he knew that to be something you had to be like Gladstone. Gladstone was the science that invented the machines, and the world run by machines like the steam turbines and boilers which made molasses, sugar and rum from a simple plant. A coolie could stay pagan and chew on the plant, or he could learn the science of the machine. To be a Gladstone-coolie was the first stage in becoming Gladstone himself. Vidia wanted to explain all this to Kampta but instead lesser words came from his mouth. 'Man, what about money?' he asked Kampta with a peasant's desperation. He wanted to ask another, more lofty question but only coolie considerations came to mind. But Kampta was not listening, withdrawing into himself again, into a little space where only he and Miriam and her brothers existed unmolested. A little space in his mind, a little space in the bush where they could plant and harvest, living as freely as the Amerindians. Free from his own people calling her a nigger whore. Free from the bleakness within which made him treat her as a nigger whore.

Vidia examined the biscuit tin that Rohini had brought home, then placed it back on the shelf, upside down so that the picture on its lid was hidden. Rohini was sleeping, her body weakened by fever. They had the range of logies to themselves. It was Diwali night and all the coolies were abroad, gathering on the plantation dam to feast. The women put on their best saris and sandals, and took up a place designated for them, far from the rumshop at the head of the dam where the men congregated. The young women sang or showed off their jewellery, their new babies; the older ones, with shabbier saris, squatted on the ground to smoke pipes, careless of the mud. They had seen enough Diwali nights, lit enough dyas of ghee and made enough prayers to Lakshmi, the goddess of wealth, to know that nothing ever changed. Still, they had had their day, let the younger ones screech and sing, those still with teeth in their mouths, those whose tattoos bearing the names of their husbands were still ostentatiously fresh on their arms. The years would pass, their teeth would slacken, and their tattoos become disfigured by the corrugation of skin, making them unreadable. How often, when their husbands beat them, or new promising men stepped off the boats, did they scratch their skin until it bled, or massaged into it home-made lotions, willing the tattoo to disappear? Or fade. But you can't expect prayers to be granted in this hop-and-drop life. No, a little fading will do, but the gods are cunning. They yield to your prayers, but by then you are nothing but an old woman squatting in plantation mud, folding your loose skin around you to stay warm, and watching across the road your husband cavorting in the rumshop, wasting money on drinks for everybody, boasting like any young man of all the fucks he did with so many mistresses and how many more he could do with the money he had hidden away from his wife. *His* wife – for however difficult to decipher, the needle-marks

128

were still there. If you put your arm before the glow of your pipe, you could still make out his name which your mother had stitched into your skin before handing you over.

Vidia stood at the door, looking out at the Diwali lights flicker and dip like fireflies. A roar went up as the men lit a huge bonfire outside the rumshop to keep them warm. He could hear the women banging stones against enamel plates to give rhythm to their song. A harmonium started up and the voices strained to follow it, the drunks bellowing out of tune or out of malice for the accomplishment of the player. Vidia felt miserable, not for himself, but for Rohini, too sick to celebrate on the one day of the year he had set aside for leisure. He had planned a special secret treat for her, a gift for all the drudgery she endured in Gladstone's kitchen to save them money for the building of their own house. They would wake up early on Diwali morning and catch a horse-cart to Port Fielding, the nearest town. He had never visited, being bound by contract to the limits of Albion estate, but on Diwali day a coolie could wander far and wide, without need of Gladstone's permission. Kampta had told him of Port Fielding, for he had worked in the plantation there. Vidia and Rohini would idle along the main thoroughfare lined with shops which Kampta described as being packed with marvellous goods. They would pause at the hardware shop to take note of the price of plates, pots, and the other utensils which would one day stock their house. They would do the same at the haberdasher's so that Rohini could choose in her mind the patterns of cloth to spread on their new bed. Afterwards they would walk by the river to watch the canoes bringing eddoes and watermelons to market. They would find a clean spot to spread a sugar-sack, picnicking on aloo roti and remembering how they made the journey across sea to Plantation Albion, like so many parcels of goods, so many bunches of plantains in a canoe, but how they were rapidly rising in value; soon they would own land and if they wanted to, set up a stall in Port Fielding market, small to begin with, but one that could grow into a proper shop with a proper signboard in proper English. When they returned home, he planned to go to the calabash tree, dig up his money and bring it back for *both* of them to count, so that they could calculate how much more they needed to save to meet the cost of their ambitions. Then they would bathe, dress, and set off for the Diwali festivities, where she would boast to the other women how far they had come, and he would buy a drink for Kampta in a flourish of generosity.

But she was sick, and he watched over her as she slept, willing her to get better. Gladstone had kept her overnight and when she came home on Diwali morning she was sick. She handed him the biscuit tin with trembling hands, as her Diwali present to him. 'Gladstone give me for all my work,' she said. 'You like the picture?' On the cover was painted a battle scene, a set of whitemen in red in one corner firing cannons, a set of whitemen in blue in the other firing back; in the middle was a field where a third set of whitemen mingled, some in blue, some in red, all on black horses, and all with raised swords. 'I feel faint,' she said, moving away towards the blanket on the floor. He dropped the tin and rushed to support her. 'Don't damage it,' she reproached him, wriggling from his grasp and lying down by her own effort.

She had brought it, she said, to put his money in, for one day his money would grow into a big pile. The glass jars were too humble, too coolie. And she had asked Gladstone to promote him, and Gladstone had promised to employ him in his counting house.

'Gladstone say what?' he asked, confused by her weakness and yet her refusal to let him touch her. But she would say no more, drawing the blanket protectively around her and turning away. He hovered over her uncertainly until she fell asleep. The biscuit tin lay damaged on the floor, one of its hinges broken. He fixed it and put it away on the shelf hurriedly, as if it didn't belong to him. He watched it sullenly, wishing she hadn't brought it to his home. It was as if Gladstone had visited unexpectedly and caught him in the midst of his poverty, a crumpled blanket on the floor, pots and pans here and there. All his intimate belongings would suddenly be exposed for what they were – meagre coolie goods. Gladstone's gaze would strip him of ambition, revealing him to be a coolie less than man, a coolie who could barely maintain his body, or his wife's, yet who planned unrealistically for a boy-child.

'Why Gladstone give you present?' Vidia asked suspiciously as soon as she awoke.

'Is only nothing, and empty, what he go to throw away.'

'He think I so low that he can pass me bruk tin,' he muttered, looking resentfully at the biscuit container. Rohini ignored him, folding the blanket neatly and putting it away. She only felt slightly better but there was much work to be done. She swept the room, lowering her head and concentrating on the floorboards to avoid Vidia's gaze. He crouched at the doorway picking idly at the flakes of skin between his toes and flicking them into the yard. His flesh was sore from some infection caught in the canefield.

'And what he say about counting house?' he asked, partly excited and partly resentful of the news.

'He say job waiting for you if you pass test.'

'Test? What test?' Vidia looked at her ignorantly.

'Test, just test, I don't know,' she replied, suppressing her irritation and gathering up some clothes to take them outside to wash. He would not budge from the doorway to allow her to pass. Just because Miriam was teaching her to read a little English didn't mean that she could come and go as she pleased. She had to answer to *him* in the end, in coolie language, not whiteman talk. He was secretly pleased though that she had learned so much in just over two years, and was proud when, a few months back, she had shown him how to write his name. A morning of blasting winds had prevented canecutting. He had come back early to find her at home, which gladdened him since she had been spending more and more time serving Gladstone. A plateful of steaming baigan-choka and rice greeted him. The storm brought on a swift darkness; they went to bed earlier than usual, and afterwards, when he had recovered his breath, she wrote the letters with her fingertips on his still breast, then erased them with provocative sweeps. 'You know how dunce I is,' he said, begging her to show him again.

They laughed then, spending most of the night practising, he tracing his name across her skin repeatedly, getting it wrong more often than not to torment her. The night was locked outside like a raging nigger and they could laugh loudly and shamelessly, knowing that their noises would not carry to their neighbours' sly coolie ears. The night and Gladstone's cane, the chained nigger and the strife, were forgotten as swiftly as he forgot the game of writing when his finger reached her nipple.

'Take back the tin to where it belong,' he ordered, removing it from the shelf and sweeping away the mark it had made in the dust. 'Why you want picture of some stupid whiteman war?' he asked, scoffing at their gloved hands wielding swords, preferring the callouses made on his by the crude handle of a cutlass.

'Man, don't fret me,' she replied, refusing to take the tin he held out. 'Throw it in the latrine if you want waste,' she said, playing cunningly on his miserly habit.

'What else Gladstone give you that I must throw in latrine?' he retaliated, hesitating at his own words which only made fitful sense.

She could have told Vidia the globe... the globe which Gladstone kept in his study, England's possessions brushed in the colour of his tongue. She brought his afternoon refreshments, placing the tray of finely cut meats on his table. He seemed unaware of her presence as usual, standing before the globe and spinning it absent-mindedly, as she often did for the sensation of forking a country with her fingers, placing its image upon her tongue and swallowing with a grace she was unaccustomed to. In the coolie hut she squatted before the plate, mashing the food into a colourful mess, before scooping it to her mouth in hasty movements. Gladstone ate with graceful cutlery, his hands carving the meat as absent-mindedly as they moved over the globe. He only behaved passionately when other men questioned his authority over the estate; or when women like Miriam used their rank methods to unhinge him. They saw him riding about the fields in an agitated mood, fingering his whip; and when the counting-house door was closed they imagined him inside, weighing and re-weighing his gold. When night came, they looked out of their logies to the Great House, waiting for its lights to go out so they could begin to laugh at him for making a fool of himself with Miriam. No wonder he was still unmarried, they gossiped, for what whitelady would go with him when the whole colony knew his degraded tastes. Only she, Rohini, appreciated the true stillness of his character, the freedom from desire which they sought to compromise, as Vidia now attempted to compromise her, thrusting the tin-can at her as if it was a measure of her worth. The tin-can was for *him* to fill with his mean coins; she brought it for *him* to gape stupidly at its picture of war, knowing that he could never understand its meaning; the best he could do was to bury it from sight under the calabash tree. At first she was as agitated as Vidia in her greed, but now she wanted nothing, as Gladstone wanted for nothing, and Kumar before him. Vidia plotted to move from the logie to his own hut, acquiring goats, chickens, and a crop of children before he died. She would not suffer like her mother Finee, feeling the weight of her husband's head in her arms as he prepared to die; a head that barely registered weight since it held few ambitions. Rohini would bear Gladstone's baby, revelling even as it burdened her with pain, swelling her body to the roundness of the globe which one day it would inherit.

PART III

MIRIAM

When Rohini tell me that she making baby with Gladstone the world stop, though I did suspect already and make plan how to survive her foolishness, because when you live among coolie you have to conspire to survive all their errors. It is not that they wrong inside themselves by Law or by how God make them, like you can say crocodile make to bite, or mongoose to chip chicken-egg, or snake to thief the life of a waterbird with one lunge and swallow. How I can explain? I want to explain but who will listen? Who believe what testimony come from Miriam mouth who only accustom to hear me bad-talk and badam-bam? When magistrate come to hear Kampta case, and after Gladstone talk big-word about how coolie does behave 'heathen and improper', I raise my hand from the crowd to talk back. Magistrate take one long look at my armpit as I raise my hand high above my head, and he sniff like magistrate them does sniff to show scorn, and he finger his spectacles like it is his rosary he is counting, or crotch he is buttoning, to keep him from evil. The tall and short and plain middle of the story is that he ignore me. *Me*, Miriam, nigger make to ignore, like how he believe coolie make to bite and break and thief. But imagine I had on a pressed black dress, and a bonnet and veil on my head, like what Mrs Aldrington used to wear to church. Imagine my black body oil and powder inside such clothes. Imagine my hair pick clean of knots and in my hand I carry handkerchief to mop my nigger-sweat as I address Mr Magistrate, for the words will come out hot. Imagine what going on: Kampta standing on the left, all proper and plantation; magistrate sitting before a desk in the middle. And me, Miriam, suddenly walk out from the crowd dressed like Miss Dignity, and making one-two graceful steps towards the magistrate – I won't wine my behind then for the corset I wear will keep it in place – and a file of papers under my shave armpit. This is how I will open, listen close everybody, hush the cutlass hacking cane, and all-you women clicking lice between your fingernails: 'In memoriam corpus fides dulce immortalis requiescat in pace.' Don't clap! Don't clap! I urge the coolies to keep their hands fresh, for I ain't done yet. Then whilst magistrate scrambling to save his glasses that slip off the end of his nose, I let go some more sweet-baby-Jesus Latin, O-find-me-and-fuck-me-on-Jordan-river-bank-and-break-my-virgin-angel-wing Latin, and then I rest my case and smile and show some scrubbed gravestone teeth. I turn to the coolie crowd and curtsey, and clapping break out like cholera epidemic they been storing up inside them for years! Truth is that magistrate will say 'guilty, guilty, guilty' and sentence Kampta to 144 extra lashes because I stir trouble, but at least somebody talk for him. And if I did talk Creole sense, who will listen? If I say that it is not Law or God but Gladstone who make Kampta behave like crocodile and mongoose and snake, not even *you* will believe, you blasted no-face no-tongue coolies. Because whiteman can't do bad, Gladstone can snare and stuff your wife like he does wildfowl, he can pepper her with bullet like he does toucan and macaw and all that God breathe paint on, then set them free to beak a seven-day sky – O how my breast does stop when I see him shove straw up their dead dripping arse and mount them in cabinets that seal out God's breath! But no, coolie still will not damn Gladstone. 'Hic! Hic! Hic!' is the only Latin that come from all-you rumshop coolie-mouth. All-you coolie mind your place like how corset mind my buttocks, it is so Gladstone stay you from complaint.

But still my heart stop for her like God heart stop when gun boom in the seven-day sky. When Rohini tell me, the world stop, God's breath in my mouth stop, and when I come to speak at last, it is only jackass-word I bray. Eee-Aaw, Eee-Aaw, Eee-Aaw. And she stare at me like a stuffed toucan trying out its glass eyes for the first time, to see what a new nigger look like.

'But you will bring tribulation upon we,' I say.

'I do what I do,' she smirk.

'But river-bank burst and the canefields sodden.'

'I do what I do.'

'But the trumpets blast Jericho, and a whale swallow Jonah,

and Daniel shit when the lion spot him, and Lot roll with daughter in the dust, and Abraham suck his nanny-goat when nobody looking, and John the Baptist beg some whore for head.'

'I do what I do.'

Coo-Coo. Coo-Coo. Coo-Coo. Gladstone preen her mouth and the girl turn bird.

So I go to Kampta to beg for help. 'She swallow massa-seed and it puff up her belly,' I say.

'Money,' he say.

'What she breed will souse the land.'

'Money.'

'A pickled child with fingers of salt.'

'Money.'

Like everybody got only one dull word, so I stop my song and box Kampta hard in the face instead. I withdraw my broth from him – my bed, my brothers, my English-tins. I banish him to regions outside my yard, where he sulk for days before hunger yoyo his belly back to me. 'How much money,' I say, for I turn into one of them.

'Twenty dollar,' Kampta say, besieging my ears with promise to take Rohini to faraway nurse to purge her belly. He dip into my bowl of plantains.

'You can't ask the nurse to owe the money?' I beg, but he turn his face and spit on the ground, making sure he swallow the plantain first.

'People don't drop baby for freeness,' he say. 'Suppose she kill Rohini by mistake? If it was me I demand thirty dollar to take risk.' He sound so bitter, as if he want to roll the white moon between his soiled fingertips.

'But for all the botheration I take for you – fan your back, douse the pain in cocoa-butter – and all the while blackman abuse me for traitoring, and you still can't risk?' I run my hand up and down his face like a blind woman recognising a counterfeit lover.

He reach for the bowl again because he know I need help and will not beat away his hand. 'Coolie deserve what they get,' he say damning himself and his tribe, 'plus, what business her baby got with you?'

Rumour will spark riot and Gladstone summon soldiery.

Coolie will agitate soon as bastard born – not because they fear for their own womanfolk, but excuse to force more wage from Gladstone. And Kampta cunning – he know I can't trust Albion midwife who does only charge Gospel price: five loaves fresh, but stale will do, and some fish. Her soul is fast but so is her tongue. No, the deed got to do in some yonder village where people won't talk because they not kin with we.

'Is *my* business,' I reply, not wanting to confess blame. When Rohini tell me I sit down to catch my breath. Right away I think that only bread-and-fish it will take to cure her, then story done, in two-three days the bleeding stop. But she let her belly fertilise, and the more I reason the more she behave wilful till I have to clamp my jaw to stop me blasting her. I sit there and watch her sift flour, and do all the kitchen work what rightly belongs to me but what she now claim because she fresh with Gladstone favours. She don't show it but I know her small heart swell in victory over a tired nigger like me who done drop many babies for Gladstone. But I stay quiet because it is me-self who encourage her to share my burden, share Gladstone. Coolie can't just come and inherit we kingdom. They got to punish like we punish, so I slacken her rope till it reach the kitchen sink and bed. If only I did strap her tight to me and mother her, but malice did sour my breast.

'You stupid more than you fat,' Kampta say, finishing the plantains and demanding a fresh bowl, 'but if you make it your business then the price is twenty dollar.'

How to find the money for my guilt? I turn coolie, firing up plot in my head, craving that God make miracle, then blaspheming when He don't and peril my soul for twenty dollar. Gladstone, like God, will not give neither, though he never deny me before when I tell him nurse-price to brush-and-cut baby. Twenty dollar now, I reason, will save you two-thousand later when the bastard born and the coolies make claim, but Gladstone holler at me how I done thief enough from his iron safe. His gullet swell and his skin turn green so before he leap me, I slip from his room and tuck my arse safe in kitchen-corner. I want the money for myself, he charge, for he never trip Rohini to make her stub her toe, and memorable vileness he so abuse me with that I blush and backtrack to the kitchen where I study how all God creation gone rotten.

Still, I search his room when his back turn, but every crease and cell clean, the iron safe too. For spite I scrape the gilt off the page edges of his books with my fingernails until I come to see the folly of my hand, gloved in gold, yet empty.

And is then Vidia walk moonless past me, his breath a blue vapour guiding him to his money. Sleep won't take me, so I leave Gladstone house and drift towards the coolie compound where Kampta settle since I chase him, pelt the bowl after him and everything else blunt in the kitchen. Kampta did stand outside my yard and snarl but he is only a puppy-dog, for when I go after him with pot-spoon, you should see him run! Now, in my troubles, I miss him and go to fetch him back, when I spy man coming. I duck in some bush and wait for him to pass but something tell me to follow, something seize my foot and raise it so that I float after him. Wet grass squirt as Vidia walk but I don't need follow the sound, I just trail behind him like his natural scent.

But story got no end until we can find a safe village, so I hitch the donkey-cart and Thomas lift Rohini and lie her dazed among bunches of green bananas which is the baby-price. I lure her to my hut and I boil cow-milk and sprinkle nigger-recipe – pieces of mara-bark which pass for cinnamon – which slave-time folk serve Missie. When Missie head slump to the table they haul it back and choke her sweetly. They raise one howl, horse-gallop into the dark to fetch Massa from some whore-house or gambling parlour. And when doctor say Missie dead from heart-failure – for not one bruise on her throat, not one sign of agony in her face and the rest of her not squishing piss, how we people so forgiving to leave her comely as Sheba – the whole plantation start hymn grief and behave like Sunday niggers, beg mercy for their laziness to her, and if only she would come back they would surrender all the brooches they thief from her.

But how times change, eh. I mix in the mara-bark and think how I doing it out of love for Rohini, yes, love, though I should hate the girl and her boat people. Slave days come back when coolie land in Albion, for they rob we of work and wage and one day will rule we. I should strangle the bitch, but when she slump to the floor I hold her face to stop it bruising. A small frighten face like when I was small and arise from Gladstone bed and see my face in his glass for the first time. 'Miriam,' Jesus call in a voice that sound like Gladstone, and I stare into the glass but only see myself. 'Miriam,' He whisper my name a second time, and when I look again, I see on myself the blood where Latin-man spear His side. I panic and run from the glass, from Gladstone's open hands and mouth, down the stairs, out of the front door, but Jesus follow me all the way to my hut, calling my name in the dark for the whole world to hear. But the twelfth time He say 'Miriam' I stop, I get mad, He gone too far. Brazenness take over, words form in my throat which I must have inherit because they sound nasty and biblical and I curse Him worse than Baal. 'Miriam' is not my name, I shout back. I ain't no Virgin Bride no more and I don't belong to Your blasted holy book and manacle. If You want call my name, call it Jaka, Abulli, Rebili – I reel off one list that sound angry and African, but in truth how they come to my mind is miracle to this day. Jesus like He back off, for since then, whenever He make to shake the chain at me, I throw my head back, stare into the dark and curse, and He soon-soon hush. Me and God make peace since, my conscience is no slave. I can ferry Rohini to where I must and when the donkey pause for strength and the wheels stop creak and God take advantage of the silence to chide me, I tell Him, 'why you don't pick on man-sin like what Gladstone and Kampta do the poor girl and me?' And I give the donkey one kick to make him whine and drown out God's answer.

'Ease up, sis,' Thomas say, and I turn on him.

'Who you eea-aaw eea-aaw to, eh, who you tell ease up?' And I wave grandpappy chisel at his face which I bring to protect we from bandits, and he too hush. Then He call my name again and I look up to see flocks of ibis ripening against my dark eye and Mary Magdalene tying her head in a shawl of jumbie-birds, for the earth is turning and the hour come when all things living, except we three, mourn their way home with their crosses.

'Sis, where you taking we?' Thomas ask.

To woman who cut black ribbons in her cheeks. Who grow plaits down to her waist.

'Sis, where you taking we?'

To woman who talk to owl and tree bat in their own tongue. Who know what root, what bark, what healing flower.

'Sis, where you taking we?'

To Old Higue. To Churile. To African spirit.

So Kampta did describe her, to scare the boys, but I done know it is the twenty dollar he trying to cajole out of me. I still give him the money because he desperate to snake away to his naked-skin Amerindians. But Eden is not *me* business, if he want rum them up and teach them how to swear in coolie and spread their legs in modern ways. Rohini is *me* business, so I let the snake go with eighteen dollar, and with the other two I hire donkey-cart to take her overnight to a safe village in search of a nurse. I drug and kidnap her and hide her among green bananas which will pay for the deadening of the child. Yes, God, I sin, and so what? You want me kneel down and scratch the dirt around Your feet like Vidia digging for his jars? Morning after I thief, I repent, I wait for night to take back the money but when I get to the spot, Vidia already reach. I hide and peep as he dip in one jar, in the next, in the next, and feel nothing. Howl, I urge, but the man sit stupidy-stupidy like he just done sex. Like coolie wedding done, the couple gone, and the throng, and the drummer sit in the empty yard, surrounded by the tablas, tired from all the play. So Vidia sit with his jars around him, tired from all the play.

And then I know my heart too done with play, that Ma not coming back, that Kampta will run away frequent, and only Gladstone I got, who keep me since I was a child and out of habit will secure my kitchen-job. My heart done with riot. I will poison Gladstone gradual over ten-fifteen years, till his hair drop out and doctor blame stress, his foot swell and doctor blame gout, and when he lie down his flesh stick to the Berbice chair, how it perspiring from my recipe, and doctor blame ague. 'Miriam, please for some water,' and 'Miriam, please for fan breeze,' is how Gladstone will beseech me then, and he will grow so dependent I can eat out his whole livestock or wipe my battie on every will in the iron safe, and all he will say is, 'Miriam, please for some fish broth.' But if the bastard come and coolie agitate, then all my freedom gone. Gladstone could rightly blame me for tempting him with Rohini, and I get dismiss, and what will happen then to

Thomas them and me? I taste too much cadbury and sweet-biscuits to go back to when Ma abscond and hunger scratch like we swallow pimpla. No, grandpappy chisel give we security, so if nurse fail, me-self will take the same tool and chip-loose the baby.

'Vidia not enough,' Rohini curl herself in my bed and cry, but when I lean over to comfort her she lunge at my face. 'I want more, Miriam, than button and biscuit-tin.'

'That is all there is,' I say, but she call me a wretch who feed kumari seeds to her mouth to make her barren. 'What name kumari seed?' I ask, holding down her arms and pushing her back to the bed. She shriek as if I about to batter her. 'Sleep,' I beg, 'please sleep,' but she will not let the story done. She rave about somebody call Rama, how she will stick needle in His eye so He can't look on her. And she curse a piece of bone she call Kumar. She say Kumar-bone is from some boar in India that the English catch and scrape the belly clean. 'What name boar? What name India? What name this and what name that?' I fire off question to distract her, to stop her grinning at me to show me one missing teeth. Suddenly she bawl, a noise so animal that right away I slap her quiet. The boys run in, but I shoo them away so they don't sight the blood. So much blood from such a slight coolie body!

Afterwards, when she sleep, I clean her up and put fresh cloth to her legs and pray that the flow will stop soon, that when she wake she will not accuse me, but see me as her own mother who deliver her from the scorn of men. 'Only think how they stone you if they did find out you was bearing Gladstone baby. Give glory to God and me that the baby purge from you and the secret keep from everybody, and Vidia.'

'He never batter me,' she sob, 'he never batter me.'

'Who never?' I ask, pressing her close to stifle Gladstone name, because I know it is Gladstone she dreaming about. I know she want to tell me that one day Gladstone sit her down and feed sweet word to her, make her feel special and give her English present, till she begin to believe that not every man is coarse. I know all this, for my first time was this. I too had a first time when he do it to me with promise and make me believe God create woman for magnificat. But there was a second time, and a third time, and the cock crow. So man stay. They grow to revile you.

'He never batter me,' she sob, pushing me away, but I done know she is like toucan Gladstone shoot and stuff and seal in glass. And I, Miriam, stare into the glass and see myself, so I shatter it to set her free. She break down and weep and call upon God for remedy, but is I, Miriam, who save her from labour, I who redeem her and send her back to her husband.

'Vidia not enough,' she whine, and when I ask her what else she want, she start blabber about war, about poisoning cow, about slaughtering Muslim, about burning down all the holy places.

'Vidia is all there is,' I urge, and I feel sorry for her when I say it, for which woman want to end up with a speck in her eye which she can't clean howsoever she pick and gouge?

She rear up at me again and start one madness till I have to shout at her that story done, Gladstone baby done. Albion is *we* land, *we* man and *we* story and *I* tell it how *I* want. I start the story and I kill it so *you*, Rohini, hush and listen, for you is only a freshly-come coolie. When *I* give you freedom to talk, then you talk, but I can wave my chisel any time and interrupt you and take over the story and keep it or throw it away. What right you have to make story? What right you have to make baby for Gladstone? Albion is a nigger, we slave and slaughter here, Albion is we story, and you coolie who only land this morning best keep quiet till you can deserve to claim a piece. Leave Gladstone for what he deserve, and for what I deserve, and go back to your coolie husband!

Still the bleeding will not stop, and the fever, so I keep her safely, rub her body in pecca oil, blend herb and syrup for her mouth. Vidia come, and I feed him lies about her sudden sickness. He go away grateful that I will give her free folk remedy because he don't have money to buy medicine from the dispensary. Next day he return with papaya for me and to thank me for what I do for Rohini. He look so feeble with misery that a prayer whisper from my heart for him. I wish him a pirate's fortune and his own counting-house, then I go back to fending off Rohini. I chew toba-seed and dab the spot on her forehead. I make up a canticle for her, about rich fields that her husband plough, orchards smiling with fruit, and a child born from sea-shell: after all the sickness of the crossing of water she will step on land plentiful with child, so long as she go back to Vidia and to India. Though all my words is empty they still swell my throat. I sing and sing, though God is deaf, for without my dream she will surely dead.

'Gwan, gwan, gwan swine-keeper, else I break your neck!' So Rohini chase Vidia back to India, even though his face force-ripe with grief. Rohini mock him that he turn man overnight when big thing happen to him – somebody thief out his money. The whole plantation give him pity, like dowry for a new bridegroom, and talk spread how a man – a man mind you, not a boy – who marry to his money now turn Mukti. 'What name Mukti?' I ask, and she tell me about recruiter who lead them to this sacrificial land.

Rohini say people bring gift of fig and melon to the hut, they seek advice on sickness or bad dream or neighbour's spite, but Vidia hand back the fruit and stare at the sky as if to calculate the best blessing. From all around people hurry to pick his mouth, and they offer bribe – eye-piece and looking-glass so he can better study the stars, pencil and paper to do the figuring – but what he bear in this season of prophecy he give away free.

Madness, Rohini say, madness: Vidia refuse to eat and people take his starvation for a holy sign, but Rohini claim it is madness. Why else he whimper under the blanket, howsoever she try to comfort him till she grow tired, abandon him and sleep. When she wake up, she say she see him in a corner scratching at the floorboards, crying for his money. She call, and he stop for a while, but the money-jumbie whisper in his head above common-sense or wife. Never mind how she reason or expose her breast, he only crouch lower and dig the ground softer till daylight come.

'I can't live with dog or holy man so I take shelter with you,' she say, coming back to my house. Barely a month pass since I stem her bleeding and send her back to Vidia, but now she return to burden me.

I tut-tut, sit her down and start comb her hair for it look like louse-pit.

'Soon morning, I hardly get two hour sleep, and pilgrims make noise at my door,' she complain.

I give her black tea to drink, how her lips dry.

'If only he take one-one coin from them and accumulate, but he refuse. I need bangle, Miriam, and my sari tear, I shame to show my face.'

I hitch my skirt and wipe her chin where the tea dribble.

'Drunk man will soil me like straw,' she cry.

I don't heed, instead I take her hand and move her to rest in my bed.

'But why I should hush?' she ask, 'is *they* who should hush, who beat down my door night and day, wanting freeness from Vidia when all his life I gain nothing from him but daabla and pot though he promise money from Kumar, money to make house. One mad-rass Mukti I marry!'

She laugh and laugh till I grow frighten and order her to quiet, like I order her to quiet when she did take me to see the pilgrims lining up to worship Vidia. The logie empty, only Vidia sitting on the doorstep counting the bones of his hand. Boy or man I can barely tell, how his body wither and I want rush to him with all my fat but Rohini hold me back.

'You got to wait your turn else the coolies will riot,' she say, pointing to the back of the line which don't exist. 'Soon you will reach the front, only seven woman before you.'

And before I can argue that nobody there, she start one conspiracy with me, reciting in my ears all their private business.

'The first one name Sumintra, Gopaul wife but she carrying Harilall child.

'After she is Ramabai who can't make baby.

'Rookmania and Surya and Chabrani come because they can't satisfy: husband threaten to sell them and whore away the money.

'Betti get only daughters and her puppa vex bad, you can see the marks.

'Aruna right foot growing extra toe, who will marry her?'

She stoop and pick up stone but I stay her hand even though the stone will only hit air. She wriggle free and pelt and it land on make-believe Aruna, though she do no wrong. Her extra toe is not her own sin but God's mocking handiwork. I nearly chide Rohini

148

for harming the innocent, when I catch myself and drag her and me away. She fight to stay, to search the ground and stone the rest of them.

'Is Gladstone spoil you, not woman,' I whisper but she won't heed. She fly at me, kick, bawl, make to dig my eye, but I fold my hands around her and press her steadfast to me, though she fine like bird-foot that could snap easily.

'Is Vidia recruit me,' she sob, 'is Vidia ruin me.'

And Vidia who all this time ignore we, like if we don't exist, hear his name call. He look up from his empty hand to the sky, then to the ground, and a sadness come to his face as if he realise he is the only meagre thread connecting the two.

'Gwan, gwan swine-keeper,' Rohini shoo him and turn to her mending.

'I leave next week,' Vidia repeat himself, looking at me for help, but what I can do? I is not her husband to cuff till she tie her bundle and follow five steps behind wherever I walk, over rooftop or through Red Sea. I is Miriam who feed her, sleep her, rub her foot with myrrh, till she can catch her mind and clear out of my space, clear out once and for all with all her coolie tragedy. I have Gladstone to tend; every day the girl stay, Gladstone thrive till it will take a vat of poison.'

'I leave next week,' Vidia repeat himself, but she ignore him, squinting at needle-eye, trying to pass it through Gladstone gold hair. He look at me again, but I ain't got strength to roll gurmit-seed with him, much less marble rock from his tomb. The only miracle I can perform is to lie on top of man or in his ear, so I take Vidia aside and suffocate him with story, of how, as soon as Rohini head ease, I will beg passage and put her on boat to India myself. I manoeuvre his mind here and there and everywhere, I drug his common sense till he take nigger-sweat for cow-bubby milk, and when he satisfy I let him out into the darkness to breathe. He depart from my yard believing in God again. I give him strength to cross water.

'Vidia gone and you will not look upon him again,' I warn her but all she concern with is poking Gladstone hair through needle-eye. 'I promise to send you at next sailing.'

Suddenly she turn her eyes on me, they bore through me as if I is cloth. Thank Jesu Thomas wake up then to go to latrine. Thanks that I get three big black man in my house, for mad people does throw one bacchanal!

'Behave yourself,' I growl.

And seven days pass. And Rohini like she smell saltwater because she busy herself for the journey. She send Thomas to catch fish, which she dry and smoke. She send Thomas to buy flour which she make into sada-roti. She send Thomas to pick coconut which she squeeze oil for Vidia hair. Thomas glad to run shop or climb tree like a dutiful slave. He born like that, he can't change. Since Kampta flee, he waste the daylight, he cough-cough at night with sleeplessness. A boy his age should hunt sex, but all he want to do is serve Rohini. I use to worry he is bugger-battie and will bring shame on my head; worry he will tumble Rohini when my back turn, but I still glad that she living with we because she give him purpose. She will not teach him to burgle and cheat, like Kampta use to do, but how to write. Thomas fetch paper to wrap her goods, and when she take pencil and write in big letters V.I.D.I.A. on the parcel, he watch every curving movement of her hand, every downstroke and dot. And she become his mother, making jilabie just for him, smoothe his bed, wash his pants. And he start plant garden again, impatient for the bora to grow so he can present her. I watch him hurry to the docks to give Vidia the parcel before he board. I put in my last repentant two-dollar, token of what I thief from him in the first place.

'Sis, what will happen to Vidia?' Thomas ask as we kneel in the garden to sow ochro seeds.

Masts and sails. Paint freshly put on, deck prepare in tar. Demerara mud give way to a free green ocean and for weeks he speed safe till the wind come in hot and stifling and the sky thicken with the colour of cochineal. Rain and hail and the top-sail adrift, tear away and fly into the darkness, sucking the rigging after it. The coolies shriek, the sailors haul useless ropes, the captain hoarse with orders which carry to nobody. Afterwards they bring the dead up to top-deck, count them, list them in a book, hand them over to woman to wash the stains and wrap in bedsheet. Coolies wail out of duty, the priest warm to his own chanting, then roll the bodies overboard, Vidia and all. No more digging. He can't make hole in water. He done.

'Sis, what will happen to Rohini?' Thomas crow, waking me early so I can bathe and eat and sweep the house and start life fresh again, for it is rest-day Sunday and though Jesus and me at war, I still bursting to hymn.

Her body young yet, it will please all man and pass into legend. 'You hear story about Albion whore?' another Kampta will ask in another century in another rumshop. Or else she will ash her face and turn catechist, calling on man not to cast stone, not to murder girl-child soon as it born, but you believe man will listen? When the Holy Spirit seize her and shudder her body on the ground, man only waiting all respectful for her blouse to rip. I wipe the sleep from my eye but still can't see what will happen to Rohini. Since Vidia gone, all day she only making up mad-people parcels, putting in goat dung, papaya skin, tamarind leaf, gurmit seed, and pieces of bone she swear is wildboar. And on each parcel she write different name, but boy only – Kissoon, Reya, Cheddi, Gopaul, Romesh, Harilall, Balgobin – all the babies she promise Vidia, the one baby she nearly bear for Gladstone. Lord, I pray, let her get better soon and get out of my yard, else I too grow madness!

'Sis, what will happen to Kampta?' Thomas crow a third time as we mend the fence to preserve what we plant from strays.

Go to yonder river and wait on the bank for him to bloat by. I pray the Amerindians revenge on him for how he betray womanfolk and me. Fish him out of the water, untie his hands and drown him again. And before you bury him, search his pockets, trouser-seam, underneath his tongue, inside his cacahole, earhole, wherever he hide the money. Bury him deeper than six foot, pile rock on top or he will break out and one morning surprise me in the hut, tilting the soup-pot to his mouth.

Thomas push his lips out but I stop him before he can 'sis' me again. Only coolie name he call. Counting-house. Canefield. Colony. Coolie will inherit everything in time, though one turn mad today, one perish at sea, one float murdered. Three wise men with gifts for the Son and the Father and Holy Ghost or for the three thieves on the Cross, all the same, all coolie. But who care for *me*? Whoever run bring me paper and string to tie parcel for all *my* dead babies? Whoever hitch cart and take me anywhere? Whoever stop me on the road as I walk carrying fish-loaves and green bananas on my own and say, 'Miriam, girl, your foot heavy, let me relieve your load. Whoever promise that when I dead he will not forsake me to some nigger-mound? Whoever promise me my own will, tie in ribbon, and every anniversary he will brush my nigger-dust off so the paper don't stink? But who dare call me stink? Who is it I hear say I stink? Answer, you coward, come down from cloud or walk water, approach howsoever and tell me to my face that I sin; that I kill Rohini baby out of jealousy; that I kill coolie when I thief his money, not for abortion but to sweeten and keep Kampta; that Ma look on me as I sleep, see the devil and run; that I seduce Gladstone with my nigger-pokey so proper lady won't do for him. Come out of your hole and heaven, but nobody answer, is only me talking but still I can't hear the echo of myself. I feel for my face, my breast, but sense forsake me, I feel for Thomas, but nothing, the fence, the hut, the yard, Peter and Joe, nothing, and I panic, I panic and I call for Gladstone – Eloi! Eloi! Eloi! – for he will always be there, and true, he come, and then I start to cry.

EPILOGUE

Miriam's grave cannot be found.

Gladstone's estate was sold on his death in 1889, the revenues passing to his nephew, William Gladstone, the British Prime Minister. Two biographies appeared in the early twentieth century, both now out of print. An engraved portrait of him as the personification of Neptune, by the English marine artist Richard Campion, was once in the collection of the Victoria and Albert Museum, London; it can no longer be traced.

Kampta never existed.

Rohini survives through a letter written in a largely indecipherable child's handwriting to her mother Finee, which was never sent. The letter confirms the existence of the character but its contents confirm the madness of that existence.

The 'Nigger mound' was excavated by a team of English anthropologists and archaeologists in 1911. No African skeletons were found. The mound is now believed to be an Amerindian (Carib) ceremonial site dating back to pre-Columbian times.

Today, in Guyana, the macaw, toucan, ibis and jumbie-bird exist on the brink of extinction. They will soon be figments of the imagination, like Kampta.

ALSO AVAILABLE FROM PEEPAL TREE

Slave Song

ISBN: 1-84523-004-3, 72pp., £7.99

Slave Song is unquestionably one of the most important collections of Caribbean/Black British poetry to have been published in the last twenty years. On its first publication in 1984 it won the Commonwealth Poetry Prize and established Dabydeen as a provocative and paradigm-shifting writer.

At the heart of *Slave Song* are the voices of African slaves and Indian labourers expressing, in a Guyanese Creole that is as far removed from Standard English as it is possible to get, their songs of defiance, of a thwarted erotic energy. But surrounding this harsh and lyrical core of Creole expression is an elaborate critical apparatus of translations (which deliberately reveal the actual untranslatability of the Creole) and a parody of the kind of critical commentary that does no more than paraphrase or at best contextualise the original poem.

It took some time for the displaced critics to recognise that this prosaic apparatus was as much part of the meaning of the whole as the poems themselves; that Dabydeen was engaged in a play of masks, an expression of his own duality and a critique of the relationship which is at the core of Caribbean writing: that between the articulate writer and the supposedly voiceless workers and peasants.

Turner

ISBN: 1-900715-68-6, pp. 84, £7.99

David Dabydeen's 'Turner' is a long narrative poem written in response to JMW Turner's celebrated painting 'Slavers Throwing Overboard the Dead & Dying'. Dabydeen's poem focuses on what is hidden in Turner's painting, the submerged head of the drowning African. In inventing a biography and the drowned man's unspoken desires, including the resisted temptation to fabricate an idyllic past, the poem brings into confrontation the wish for renewal and the inescapable stains of history, including the meaning of Turner's painting.

'Turner' was described Caryl Phillips as 'a major poem, full of lyricism and compassion, which gracefully shoulders the burden of history and introduces us to voices from the past whose voices we have all inherited', and by Hanif Kureishi as 'Magnificent, vivid and original. The best long poem I've read in years.'

The Intended
ISBN 1-84523-013-2, £8.99

The narrator of *The Intended* is twelve when he leaves rural Guyana to come to England. There he is abandoned into social care, but with determination and self-discipline seizes every opportunity to follow his aunt's farewell advice: '...but you must tek education...pass plenty exam'. With a scholarship to Oxford, and an upper-class white fiancée, he has unquestionably arrived, but at the cost of ignoring the other part of his aunt's farewell: 'you is we, remember you is we.' At one level a moving semi-autobiographical novel, *The Intended* is also a sophisticated postcolonial text with its echoes of *Heart of Darkness*, its play with language and its exploration of the instability of identity. As an Indo-Guyanese, the narrator is seen as a 'Paki' by the English, as some mongrel hybrid by 'real' Asians from India and Pakistan; and as sharing a common British 'Blackness' whilst acutely conscious of the real cultural divisions between Guyanese of African and Indian origins.

Disappearance
ISBN 1-84523-014-0, £8.99

A young Afro-Guyanese engineer comes to a coastal Kentish village as part of a project to shore up its crumbling sea-defences. He boards with an old English woman, Mrs Rutherford, and through his relationship with her discovers that beneath the apparent placidity and essential Englishness of this village, violence and raw emotions are latent, along with echoes of the imperial past. In the process, he is forced to reconsider his perceptions of himself and his native Guyana, and in particular question his engineer's certainties in the primacy of the empirical and the rational.

This richly intertextual novel uses references to the work of Conrad, Wilson Harris and VS Naipaul to set up a multi-layered dialogue concerning the nature of Englishness, the legacy of Empire and different perspectives on the nature of history and reality.

Ed. Kevin Grant
The Art of David Dabydeen
ISBN: 1-900715-10-4, pp. 231, £12.99
In this volume, leading scholars from Europe, North America and the Caribbean discuss his poetry and fiction in the context of the politics and culture of Britain and the Caribbean. These studies explore David Dabydeen's concern with the plurality of Caribbean experience; the dislocation of slavery and indenture; migration and the consequent divisions in the Caribbean psyche. In particular, these essays focus on Dabydeen's aesthetic practice as a consciously post-colonial writer; his exploration of the contrasts between rural creole and standard English and their different world visions; the power of language to subvert accepted realities; his use of multiple masks as ways of dealing with issues of identity and the use of destabilizing techniques in the narrative strategies he employs.

Bruce King writes in *World Literature Today*: 'This is ... an extremely useful work consisting of three interviews and nine essays on the subject's poetry and novels, followed by a bibliography of books and articles by Dabydeen and a list of reviews of his creative work. Part of the usefulness is that the essays overlap, build on, and disagree with one another. They bring out Dabydeen's recurring themes, autobiographical material, and the links among his scholarly publications, interviews, and creative writings.'

Ed. Lynne Macedo and Kampta Karran
No Land, No Mother: Essays on the Work of David Dabydeen
ISBN: 1-84523-020-5, pp. 240, £14.99
In these essays, dialogue across diversity and the simultaneous habitation of multiple arenas are seen as dominant characerics of Dabydeen's work. Essays by Aleid Fokkema, Tobias Doring, Heike Harting and Madina Tlostanova provide rewardingly complex readings of Dabydeen's *Turner*, locating it within a revived tradition of Caribbean epic (with reference to Walcott, Glissant and Arion), as subverting and appropriating the romantic aesthetics of the sublime and in the connections between the concept of terror in both Turner's painting and in Fanon's classic works on colonisation. Lee Jenkins and Pumla Gqola explore Dabydeen's fondness for intertextual reference, with the nature of canonic authority and ideas about the masculine. Michael Mitchell, Mark Stein, Christine Pagnoulle and Gail Low focus Dabydeen's more recent fiction, *Disappearance, A Harlot's Progress* and *The Counting House*. By dealing with his more recent work and looking more closely at Dabydeen's Indo-Guyanese background this collection complements the earlier *Art of David Dabydeen*.

Buy these and others of our over two hundred Caribbean and Black British titles from our bookstore at: peepaltreepress.com.

Contact hannah@peepaltreepress.com or phone +44 (0)113 245 1703, or write to 17 King's Avenue, Leeds LS6 1QS, UK

In the UK, titles are distributed by Central Books (tel. 0845 4589911)

In the USA by Independent Publishers Group (tel. 312 337 0747/ email frontdesk@ipgbook.com)

In the Caribbean by David Williams: (email intermediaamericana@compuserve.com)